This book is a work of fiction and any resemblances to persons, living or dead, places, events, or locales is purely coincidental. They are productions of the author's imagination and are used fictitiously.

Published by Richard Stephenson.

http://www.richardstephenson.net/

Cover Art produced by Laura Wright LaRoche at LLPix Photography.
http://www.llpix.com/

For Irene

"Hope is being able to see that there is light despite all of the darkness."
Archbishop Desmond Tutu (1931-   )

"The world wants to be deceived, so let it be deceived."
Petronius (27-66)

"Too much knowing causes misery."
Lorenzo de' Medici (1449-1492)

Part 1 - 2038
Eleven years after the collapse
Four years after the Chinese War

CHAPTER ONE

"It is in the darkest of times that our faith is put to the test my dear brothers and sisters. In the face of suffering and death, the Lord may seem absent from our lives, but fear not, he will never forsake his children. All of us, every single one of us, have lost precious loved ones since this all began. We must have faith; above all we must trust that our heavenly father will protect those who believe in His love."

Father Nathan Elias paused and looked upon his congregation. The words he just spoke felt like a lie. He scanned the faces in the crowd, some looking back at him, others looking in his direction but not really looking at him. Nathan wished that someone would shout out that God didn't exist or He was simply looking the other way while His creation destroyed itself. Such a distraction would be a refreshing change of pace.

"You know, I have to be honest with you, it's hard for me at times to believe in what I'm saying. I'm not perfect, I'm the same as you, I have doubts, I struggle with my faith." Father Elias paused, not really knowing what to say next as he seldom went off script. His confession had a powerful effect as every eye in the sanctuary was locked on him, shocked by such brutal honesty. "Four years? Doesn't it feel like forty? I have to remind myself every day that what feels like a lifetime has only been four years. We've lost so much and have so little to show for it. I'm sure many of us thought that The Pulse would be the most horrific event of our lives. I clung to hope that if we persevered and remained strong that we would survive. I prayed every night for our safety and that God would deliver us from despair." Nathan closed his eyes as he felt a wave of anger wash over him. Anger is what had held his tongue for so long. He was venturing into dangerous territory and feared his words would be destructive to the very people that counted on him for guidance and stability. He pushed on, hoping the God would guide him. "Then, something that we never dreamed would happen in our lifetime found its way to our very homes – war. I always considered Howard Beck to be the greatest man of our time. After the PSA saved us from annihilation I thought salvation had come at last." Father Elias didn't realize it, but his voice had risen considerably. "Was it over? Had our patience finally paid off? Did our lives finally have some semblance of peace? No! It did not! We had no choice but to sit back and watch as the Chinese tried to take everything from us! Oh, we fought them with everything we had, we gave up everything for victory … and that's exactly what we paid – everything!" Nathan felt as though a weight had been lifted, he had waited for so long to unburden himself from this torment. His rage subsided as he saw tears on the cheeks of several faces in the dirty pews in front of him. Shame overwhelmed the priest for his selfish indulgence.

Fear quickly replaced shame in the form of an unfamiliar face. Only Nathan saw the disheveled man quietly enter the church and sit on the back pew. A combination of death and a lack of faith had diminished the size of the congregation. Three hundred people had once filled twenty rows. Now Father Elias' flock could comfortably occupy the first five rows, which they currently did. Someone other than Father Nathan would notice the stranger only if they turned around in their seat.

"Faith. The only thing we can cling to in these desperate times is our faith in the Lord. Let's face it; it's all we have left. We are being presented with the ultimate test of our faith. I am not a prophet, but I personally believe that we have all just walked off the Ark with Noah. God has wiped the wicked off the face of the earth. The old ways of greed and corruption doomed us. When we stopped loving our neighbor as ourselves we guaranteed our own failure. I don't pretend to make sense of any of this. I know as well as all of you that men and women of faith, people who feared the Lord suffered horribly. We must have faith that it was all part of God's plan. I believe that that the slate has been wiped clean. We have been given a chance to start anew. God has torn down the old world, the wicked one, so that we can build a new one in His name."

Father Elias saw smiling faces and returned them with his own. He glanced to the back row only to find the stranger was missing. Had he imagined the lost soul? He quickly dismissed the odd interruption and closed out his message with a prayer. When he said amen, the congregation rose to sing the closing song.

The weary parishioners slowly shuffled out of the run-down building. Many of them walked the short distance to their homes; others mounted horses for a longer journey. Father Elias remained in the church as he had every Sunday for many years. The distant memory of having a fiscal budget that allowed for a janitorial staff had long left his mind. He didn't mind spending his Sunday afternoons cleaning the church building. With water being in scarce supply, the luxury of mopping the floors only arrived when he could collect rainwater. He had been looking forward to his cleaning session all week. The town's scout team had gone on its weekly supply run and brought Father Elias a gift – a can of Pledge. With dust rag in hand, Nathan eyed the dusty podium.

"You ready for a proper polish old friend?"

Nathan ascended the stage and began wiping down the lectern with care. The door at the rear of the auditorium slowly creaked open to reveal the stranger that had occupied the back row during the service. The priest eyed the man with fear. Father Elias was seventy-three years old and while he was in good health, he did not come close to having the strength of the man that was sure to be half his age. Nathan dismissed fears of violence, judging a man on his appearance had always been one of his shortcomings. However, in this case, any rational person would be struck by fear at the sight of this man. He was tall, muscular, and had the most intense eyes Nathan had ever seen. His clothing was in tatters barely clinging to his body and his feet were absent shoes. The sun had harshly weathered his face. The priest could easily dismiss all of this if it weren't for the fact that the stranger's hands and forearms were covered in dried blood.

The man slowly walked down the aisle towards the

priest. Nathan studied the poor soul and could not determine his intentions. It was almost as though the man had no idea where he was or what he was doing. Father Elias nervously cleared his throat. "Are you hurt, young man? Do you need help?"

The stranger did not reply and continued walking down the aisle.

"Mister, you don't look so good. Are you hungry? I don't have any food here, but I'd be pleased to have you over to my house and eat lunch with you. How does that sound?"

The man did not speak, but for the first time looked the priest in the eye with a vacant stare.

"Son, what brings you here? How can I help you?"

The wanderer ignored Father Elias, sat down in the front row and studied the statue of a crucified Jesus behind the pulpit.

The elderly priest turned around to see what the mysterious newcomer was gazing upon. "Do you know God's grace, my son? Is it redemption you seek?"

For the first time, the filthy man seemed to be in the here and now. He locked eyes with Nathan and for the first time in as long as he could remember, spoke to another human being. His voice was raspy. "What did you say?"

Father Elias slowly descended the short staircase and stood directly in front of the troubled man. "Redemption. Are you lost, my son?"

The stranger looked into the caring eyes of the priest, searching for something to say. After he was able to escape the grasp of crushing despair, he closed his tear filled eyes and spoke. "Nothing can redeem my sins; I'm responsible for all of this. It's all my fault."

"No, no, no my son. Christ paid the price for all of us; nothing you can do or ever could have done precludes you from his salvation. You only need to ask forgiveness and believe in the saving power of his grace."

"If you only knew."

"What is it you are responsible for? What burden

do you carry that is so heavy? Let Christ take that burden from you."

"This. All of this, everything. It's because of me."

The priest knelt before the man and took his hands into his. "Whatever it is you think you are responsible for, I promise you the Lord will forgive you. I'll be with you as you take the first steps into a new life. Begin a new journey today and leave your old life behind."

The priest slowly freed his hands and sat down next to the man. Father Elias retrieved a handkerchief from his pocket and slowly cleaned the dried blood from his fingers. The man noticed and was grateful for the priest's kind discretion. "Are you going to ask me about the blood?"

"Do you want to tell me?"

"I'd rather not."

"Is it the reason you came here today?"

"No."

"Why are you here, my son?"

"Do you really believe what you said today? You think all of this is a part of God's plan for us? To start over?"

"I do, yes."

"You really have faith in his hell we live in? Sorry, I probably shouldn't use that kind of language."

"It's quite all right; I would say you're not too far off the mark."

"You're pretty brave for a priest."

"Why? Because I have faith?"

"No, because you didn't turn me away. I know how I look. Figured you'd be afraid of me."

"I spent a lot of years being afraid. At my age, it's a waste of time to fear death. If today is the day, then so be it. I'm ready to go home when the Lord calls on me." The two men sat in silence for a brief moment. Father Elias decided it was time to get to the point of this bizarre visit. "Why are you here, my son? You must have a reason. Let me know what it is and maybe I can help."

"I don't know what to do, Father. I've tried everything."

"Tried what?"

"It was my job to keep everyone safe and I failed."

"Keep who safe?"

"Everyone. I can make it right. I know I can. I just need more time."

"I'm afraid I don't understand, my son. Maybe you should start from the beginning."

"I wouldn't know where to begin."

"How about we start with your name and go from there."

"My name is Richard. Richard Dupree."

CHAPTER TWO

Maxwell Harris kicked back a shot of vodka, letting it burn all the way down. It was almost three in the morning and the prospect of getting some sleep from passing out drunk was appealing. Max had a healthy supply of Ambien to fall back on; however, the local neighborhood drugstore didn't have any in stock. In fact, the local neighborhood drugstore had gone without pretty much every drug known to man for many years, as had every pharmacy in the country. The shelves of most commercial ventures had been picked clean during the previous four years. The occasional Mom 'n Pop store in the middle of nowhere became a goldmine for Max's scout teams. The one hundred eighty pills of Ambien hadn't been found in one of those goldmines, but rather in an abandoned home. Husband and wife both had prescriptions, which was fortunate for Max. Chronic pain still haunted Max as it had for decades and Ambien was the only means to decent slumber.

Another shot disappeared down Max's throat. He stood up and retrieved a box of matches to light the kerosene lamp on the dresser of his dirty home. He fumbled to retrieve his boots from the floor and ending up dropping one of them. Max looked back at the bed and saw his wife stirring.

"Honey, where are you going? It's the middle of the night."

"Shit. I'm uhhh, just goin' fur walk."

"And you're drunk, again. Nice."

"Oh shut up, not drunk. Take it easy, just gobacksleep."

"You are drunk. You can barely talk."

"Gimme a break. Always on my case. Sheesh!"

"Just don't do anything stupid, please. These people look to you as their leader."

Max laughed. "Leader of what exactly? I *was* the leader of something that mattered. The 'people' you talkin' 'bout out there are the only morons too dumb to haul ass away from here like the restofem." Max clumsily put on the first boot and then fell to the floor putting on the second. He laid there on the floor laughing.

Elizabeth Harris rolled over, not wishing to engage her drunken husband. "Just don't do anything stupid."

Max stood up and swayed back and forth for a few seconds. Once he had his bearings, he looked towards the bed. "Yeah, yeah, yeah. Just take it easy for once in your life, go back to sleep." Max stumbled to the front door and stood in the doorway. A blast of cold air sharpened his senses and straightened his walk. With the aide of his cane, Max strolled down the path to the north tower of the compound and climbed the ladder.

"What's up, boss?"

"Can't sleep. What was your name again?"

"Harry."

"That's right. You and your brother joined us … a month ago?"

"Yeah, something like that."

"Anything going on out there?" Max looked past the perimeter towards the tree line.

"Not a thing. Kinda creeps me out not seeing any wildlife. You'd think you'd see raccoons or squirrels or something. Just … nothing."

"Lots of terrible shit happened here. This place is cursed."

"What did happen here? No one will really give me a straight answer."

Max hadn't spoken about that fateful day four years ago to anyone, not even his wife. Elizabeth tried at first to get him to open up about it, but quickly realized it was a subject that was better left alone. "Let me ask you something, Harry. What have you heard?"

"The only consistent thing people say is to not bring it up with you."

"I'm not surprised. What else?"

"I'm not sure if I believe it, but a few people said the Chinese War ended here."

"Yeah, I guess you could say that."

"So why is that so terrible? We fought them on our own soil for six long years and we won."

"You seriously believe that?"

"Don't see any Chinamen around trying to kill me, so, yeah, I do. How do you see it?"

"Kinda like a guy burning down his own house to stop a burglar and saying he came out on top." Max glared into Harry's eyes, daring him to disagree.

"Never really thought of it like that. Can't really say I can have an educated discussion on the matter. Like most people I had no idea what was at stake or how it could have played out one way or the other. All I know is the Chinese are gone and that can't be all bad. You would know a lot more than me, not gonna argue that. I mean, after all, you were a pretty big deal. You were close with Howard Beck from the start and served as vice-president when his son was running the PSA."

"Those days are over."

"Is that why you're so pissed off? You want to be some big politician again?"

Max balled up his fists and gritted his teeth. "You'd better choose your words carefully."

Harry laughed. "Or what? Whaddya gonna do? Half crippled drunks shouldn't make threats. Look man, take it easy. You haven't exactly cornered the market on suffering and loss. We're all in this together. I'm on your side."

Max looked upon Harry's smiling face and relaxed. "You're right. Truth is I hated politics, probably as much as Howard."

"Then what is it? Why does everyone walk on eggshells around you?"

Max paused and looked up at the moon, deep in thought. A moment passed by and he looked at Harry. "Have a good night, my friend." Without another word, Max climbed down the ladder and stumbled away.

Max felt his inebriation slipping away and would have no part of it. He clawed at his jacket pocket and retrieved his flask. The comforting burn of vodka on his throat solved all his problems, or at least silenced them for the time being. Max needed to do something productive to distract him from the exchange he had just had with

Harry. As worthless as he felt, he was still the leader of the makeshift camp that had been hastily built after the war ended. After it was all over, he just didn't have the will or the strength to relocate. What started out as a dozen traumatized people clinging to each other for support slowly grew into a community of close to a thousand. Max never volunteered or showed interest in being their leader; everyone just naturally looked to him given his status as vice-president of the Pacific States of America during its short existence.

Max did have a purpose in life that kept him driven. It wasn't his community, it wasn't his health, which was rapidly declining thanks to his constant state of intoxication, and it wasn't even his marriage. The reason he got out of bed in the morning was to right the things that had been done wrong on that day four years ago. Max deluded himself into thinking his quest was that of justice when in reality it was pure vengeance.

Max walked to the front gate of the compound in the hopes that the two men standing guard there would be asleep at their post. He was still filled with rage over Harry bringing such painful memories to the surface and he was looking to take it out on someone. Max wanted to punch him in the face for being so nosy but couldn't fault the man for being naturally curious. Chewing out the guards would satisfy the need. As he got closer to the gate he saw that his needs would not be fulfilled, as the two men were standing ready with their rifles just as they should be.

"Mornin', boss, you're up early."

"Yeah, Andy, can't really say I woke up. Never really went to sleep."

"That sucks."

"Anything going on?"

"Naw, been quiet. Quiet for the past few days. Last week's excitement seemed to be a one-time thing. I thought for sure they'd be back but looks like you were right."

"Well, you could end up being right, that's why we have to remain vigilant. Six guys lookin' to storm our gates and take what's ours can just as easily be a scouting party for a much larger force. If we're lucky, it was just the six guys that we scared into never coming back."

"We'll be ready. Scumbags 'round here know not to fuck with us. We've proven it every time."

"That we have, Andy, that we have." Max smiled for the first time in days. His smile quickly faded as he looked down the long road leading to the front gate. Andy and his silent partner followed Max's stare.

"We have anybody out?"

"No, boss, the recon team made it back around midnight. Everyone's accounted for."

"Your eyes are better than mine, how far out do they look?" Max lied, he had perfect vision but his drunk, blurry eyes couldn't focus.

"I'd say a mile at least." Andy grabbed his binoculars and studied the coming threat. "I count four torches. Two on horseback, two walking, hard to make out but maybe three more walking behind them. Say ten of them to be on the safe side."

Max kept his eyes on the dim light and spoke to Andy's partner. "Whoever's on standby, wake 'em up and get their asses up here quick. We got maybe eight minutes before they're in shooting range."

"I'm on it, boss." Max couldn't remember the fellow's name but admired his sense of urgency. Four and a half minutes later the standby squad of twelve was in full gear ready to take orders from Max. "Three snipers on the gate tower, go!" The three men did not hesitate and up the stairs they went. "I want a two man team in the north tower and another two man team in the west tower, go!" Like before, the men were accustomed to quickly following directions and smartly went about carrying them out. Max looked around at the remaining five members of the standby squad. "The rest of you men, stay right here with me and Andy when we greet our new visitors. Remember, no one does a damned thing unless I say so or they fire off the first round. After that, kill every last one them."

"Uh, Boss, you might wanna get up here," said

Andy.

Max climbed the ladder to the gate tower. "What? What is it, Andy?"

"See for yourself." Andy handed Max the binoculars. Max's eyes were blurry, but could still make out what Andy was talking about. He counted two on top of an SUV being pulled by horses, two walking with torches, and at least two dozen men walking behind the procession. "Son of a bitch. Sound the alarm! Somebody sound the fucking alarm! Now!" Before Max could finish swearing, the large bell relocated from the church steeple to the front gate tower was being violently rocked back and forth. The racket it made was deafening. In thirty seconds, close to a hundred soldiers were in the streets ready to defend the makeshift walls of their compound.

Max stood atop the gate tower with his arms spread wide, like a shepherd gathering his flock close to him. "Calm down everyone, just calm down! We've done this before many times and this time is no different. Everyone remember your training and focus. Watch each other's backs and we'll survive. We still have a wall protecting us so let's not get too excited."

"Andy! Get over here!" Andy ran from the front of the gate tower towards Max to receive instruction. "Andy, these car batteries better have juice in them. Tell me you tested the spotlight, Andy. Andy! Tell me you tested these batteries and tell me fucking spotlights work!"

"Yeah, boss, yeah, of course they work. We test it every night an hour after the sun goes down. You're good to go, I swear it."

"All right then, Andy, they're close enough I think. Let's shine some light on this party."

A bank of twelve car batteries had been daisy-chained together to power three large spotlights that were each four feet across. All three were aimed at the coming caravan.

"Now, Mr. Cordero," said Max.

Andy flipped the switch and three hundred yards away the approaching convoy stopped, blinded and disoriented from the lights.

Max drew in a deep breath. "Drop your guns! Do it now! Drop 'em! One of you raises a gun and you all die!"

The men stopped and carefully placed their guns on the ground. One of the men on top of the SUV decided to speak for the group. "Max? Are you Max? What the hell is this, man? I was told you're a reasonable guy that we could trust!"

Max turned to Andy. "Well, this is an unexpected turn of events. You know this clown?"

"Never laid eyes on the man."

"He seems to know me."

"Of course he knows you, you're a celebrity. Everyone knows you."

"Shut the hell up, funny man."

"Why don't you stop busting my balls and ask the man himself?"

"Good idea, hadn't thought of that, knew I kept you around for something." Max sarcastically patted Andy's arm and turned his attention to the man that had just spoken. "Whatever game it is you're playing you can cut the shit right now. We're not opening our gates. If you're looking for a place to raid for supplies, you've come to the wrong place my friend. And all of you, keep your hands where we can see them!"

"Look, Max, it's not like that. We don't want anything from you and we mean you no harm. We have a man here that has come a long way to make it back home to you."

"Bullshit. Everyone we know is inside these walls."

"Theodore Forrest."

Max rolled his eyes. "Again, bullshit. He's been dead a long time."

"No bullshit. I'm telling the truth. He's here in the SUV."

"Assuming you're telling the truth, why isn't he talking to me? Is he your hostage? Is that was this is? You want a ransom?"

"Theo is my friend, my brother. We went through hell to get him here and lost a few good men along the way. He's very sick. It hurts me to say it but he'll be dead soon. He's been barely holding on just to deliver a message to you. He won't tell me what it is, says he'll only speak to you. Now cut the paranoid bullshit and get down here and see for yourself. Keep your guns on us if that makes you feel better. None of us will move a muscle, you have my word."

Max turned to Andy. "I'm going down. Get word to the snipers to stay locked on target and not to do anything unless they make the first move."

"You're actually buying this nonsense? This smells like a trap."

"Andy, we either shoot them all dead right now or we play this out. If Theo really is in that SUV, don't think he'd appreciate us killing his friends."

"Still don't like it."

"Me neither. Oh, and Andy?"

"Yeah, boss?"

"Make sure the horses aren't shot, we need 'em."

"Funny."

"Not joking. Walking sucks, especially for me."

"Don't shoot the horses, got it."

Max climbed down the ladder to meet his nervous wife. "Max, what's going on? Who is it? Are we safe?"

"It's under control. Just a group of con-artists saying they're bringing Theo home to us."

"You told me Theo was dead."

"He is dead. A trusted source confirmed as much."

"What are going to do?"

"Gonna play their game for now."

"Wait. You're not going out there, are you?"

"Relax. We disarmed them and have them in our scopes. One false move and …"

"You're gonna kill them? Just gun them down like animals? What if they're good people?"

"If they're good people we won't have to shoot them."

"You know it's not that simple. Good people get nervous and make mistakes."

"And I'm not letting one of our people die over a mistake. If it comes down to us versus them …"

"I'm coming with you."

"What? Elizabeth, I don't have time for …"

"Let's go, come on."

Elizabeth Harris was a stubborn woman. Max knew the only reason she was tagging along was so the strangers would stand a better chance of survival. She knew her presence would calm itchy trigger fingers. Justified or not, anyone firing off a shot and jeopardizing the safety of the big man's wife would sorely regret it.

"Fine. But you and I need to have a talk."

"Sure, when you're sober, which will probably be, uh, never."

"I'm sober. Well, kinda."

The front gate opened a few feet to allow Max and Elizabeth to immerge. They walked down the narrow road and stood a safe distance from the SUV. Max ignored the SUV and studied the faces of everyone in the group for signs of deception. Everyone seemed calm and cooperative.

The leader of the group climbed down from the roof of the SUV and offered his hand to Max. "Mr. Harris, I'm Isaac Lynwood. We've come a long way to meet you."

"Keep your hands where we can see them and pay more attention to the men on the wall with the guns pointed at you."

"Fair enough."

"Okay, I'm here. Bring this man you think is Theodore Forrest out so I can see him."

"I'm afraid that's not possible. He's very weak and we shouldn't move him."

"So you want me to climb in the back of an SUV? You think I'm stupid? I have no intention of being a hostage."

"Max, please. You have to trust me on this. Theo wants to see his wife Vanessa and his son James before he passes. He fought for you in the war and wants to be buried here next to Captain Tullos and Lieutenant Barry."

Max hadn't for one second entertained the possibility that any of this was true. The anger and distrust in his eyes faded. Max's mouth fell open and his wife had to prop him up to keep him from falling over.

"They saved his life, Max. But you already know that, don't you? Please, we don't have much time."

Max fought back tears. "He's alive? He's really in there?"

"Yes, and he has something very important to tell you." Isaac looked to one of his men and nodded his head. The rear door of the SUV rose. Holding his wife's hand, Max slowly walked around and looked inside.

"Theo, is that you?"

"Yes, old friend, it's me. I've come a long way to tell you, Maxwell, that our old friend is up to no good and you have to stop him."

CHAPTER THREE

A tall, gray-haired man in a four thousand dollar tailored suit stood outside a dilapidated shack that was trying to pass itself off as a café. He had never been a fan of St. Louis but in his travels he'd been in far worse places. He felt the eyes of everyone on the street studying him. He couldn't have been more out of place surrounded by abject poverty. No one, including pickpockets and muggers, dared approach him. Even though he was in his seventies, he projected a sense of danger that few would dare attempt to breach.

He scanned both ends of the busy street and walked around to the rear of the shack to inspect the exit, as had been the custom in his line of work for five decades. Satisfied with his possible route of egress, he circled back around to the front of the café and checked his watch. He had one hour before his meeting. Plenty of time to find a dining establishment that far exceeded the one he was currently surveying.

An hour and ten minutes later two men occupied a table in the dilapidated shack. They also stood out in stark contrast to their environment. They wore clean clothes, were well groomed, and were physically fit.

"How good is this guy?"

"The best."

"Says who?"

"You really don't know?"

"By all means, enlighten me."

"The guy's a legend. Word around the campfire is he's the best. The guy's a ghost; he's done some pretty amazing things the past few years."

"Like what?"

"Who do you think brought down the Unified American Empire?"

"Well, popular opinion says the Pacific States of America."

"Afraid not. He was responsible for the deaths of six of the regional governors, and then he delivered President Sterling and Jackson Butler to the PSA."

"Horseshit."

"It's true, he was also responsible for hacking into Howard Beck's computer and bringing down the PSA's defenses long enough for the Chinese to get a foothold into America. Beck's robots and drones were fighting on the side of the Chinese for a short period, gave them the advantage at the start of the war."

"You're telling me one guy did all of that?"

"I am."

"How will we know when he gets here? He's already ten minutes late. What does he look like?"

"I have no idea."

"Wait. You mean we don't even have a picture of this guy?"

"I'm not sure one exists. Remember, he's a ghost."

"I think that's him."

Both men looked to the doorway to find a stoic looking man scanning the café. His demeanor was intense but calm. It was as though a predator had walked in and was scanning for prey. Once his steely gaze landed on them, he immediately knew they were the men he was looking for and slowly approached them with the cordialness of a butler.

"May I join you?"

One of the men glared at him. "That depends, you have an appointment?"

The older gentleman let the rudeness sink in and while his eyes conveyed contempt, he smiled. "Yes, I believe I do."

"Please, sit down, I'm Frank, this is Willie."

Knowing the most intimate details of both of the men's lives, the silver-haired man pretended that he just heard their names for the first time. Once he had wiped down the filthy seat with a handkerchief, he sat down. "You may call me Charles."

Frank continued, "Charles, what brings you to our fine city?"

"No offense intended, my good man, but what's left of this city does not warrant compliment."

"It all depends on how you look at it. St. Louis ain't no tourist attraction anymore but it's the place men like you come to when you they're looking for information or need a job done."

"Men like me? And what sort of man am I exactly?"

"The type of man that seeks out a man like me."

"Well said, sir. Let's get down to business. I have been led to believe that you have at your disposal a team of highly specialized operatives. Ex-special forces, former law enforcement, highly trained individuals, is that correct?"

"I do. How many do you need?"

"Twelve."

"That can be arranged."

"Excellent."

"What type of job are we talking about?"

"That all depends if you can deliver on my next request."

"I'm all ears."

"I require someone with a high level of technical expertise."

Frank stared at Charles for a few seconds and once he realized the request was serious, burst into laughter. "To do what exactly? We've been living in the Stone Age for the last four years. What's the matter? Generator on the fritz?"

Charles was not amused. "If such a task is too difficult for you …"

"Whoa, slow down. Just relax. I have just the guy in mind. About your age, used to be a big shot back in the day. Worked for one of those places with a bunch of letters, something to do with going into space."

"NASA."

"Yeah, that's it! You've heard of it?"

Charles was beginning to have doubts. "I'm surprised you haven't."

"I only made it to the third grade before they made folks pay for their kids to go to school. Got two brothers. No way my mom could pay for three kids to go to school.

It was free one year then not the next. Mom always said that was when things started going downhill for good. Wasn't long after that only thing we worried about was having food and going to school wasn't even a thought."

"Such a shame. I must say I agree with your dear mother's assessment. When can I meet with this gentleman? After I'm certain he possesses the skill set I require we can move forward."

"Let's not get ahead of ourselves. Before I arrange a meet I wanna talk payment. Not wasting my time if it's not gonna be worth my while."

"Suffice it to say your payment will be substantial."

"How substantial?"

"Not only will you compensated twice your standard rate in silver, you will have enough power and influence to take your enterprise to a level you never dreamed possible."

"I like the sound of that. It'll take time to fetch your man. I can have him here in time for dinner tomorrow."

"I wasn't anticipating such a long wait, but that is acceptable."

"Like I said, Stone Age, bicycles and horses are the fastest way to get around. Last I checked, the local gas stations aren't expecting new tankers to show up and fill the pumps."

"If my operation goes as planned, that might change."

"No shit? Really?"

Charles frowned. "Please do not use vulgarity, I find it distasteful."

"What's the big deal? You a preacher or something?"

"Far from it. I'm a gentleman that prefers civility."

"Whatever, man. I'm cool. You wanna hang for the night? Get you a room, set you up with some girls, on the house."

"Your hospitality is appreciated, but I must decline. I will meet you here at 5pm tomorrow."

"That'll work. We should have him here by then.

Sure you don't wanna stay? No one's gonna judge if you prefer boys. We got plenty of both."

"I'll be fine, thank you."

"Suit yourself."

Charles stood up and straightened his tie. "Gentlemen, until tomorrow."

Frank and Willie remained seated and watched the old man leave in disgust.

Frank could feel Willie staring at him. "Something on your mind? Spit it out."

"I don't trust him."

"Shut up, you don't trust anyone, me included."

"No, I'm serious, that guy's trouble. No one turns down free ass. Any man don't wanna bust a nut ain't right in my book."

"Give the guy a break. He's an old man that probably can't get it up anymore."

"Something about him just don't sit right with me. He'll double cross us first chance he gets."

"Hey, this is a good thing, don't screw it up."

"Relax, I'm just gonna follow him and see what he does. Maybe get him out of his room and search his stuff."

"He'll kill you if you get caught. Just leave it alone."

"Stop treating me like a rookie. Been doin' this a lot longer than you. I know what I'm doing." Willie was already finished with the conversation by the time he made it to the door.

Frank yelled toward the door. "Tell you what, you fuck this up and I'll kill you myself."

Willie spotted Charles at the other end of the square and followed him, keeping him in his line of sight. Willie was a former St. Louis homicide detective and knew the city like the back of his hand. Prior to the collapse of 2027, the national crime rate was at an all-time high. Willie had watched year after year as the budget dried up and more and more detectives were laid off. Homicides in major cities were so commonplace that the victims' families didn't really expect justice unless the murder happened in full view of witnesses and the fingerprint laden murder weapon was left behind. Two wars and eleven years later found the once great city of St. Louis a hollow shell of its former self.

Judging by the direction he was walking, Willie deduced that the old man was headed to the Blue Goose, one of Willie's more popular hotel and bar known to provide companionship to weary travelers. Willie stood a block away and lit a cigarette, watching the mysterious man enter the bar. A few minutes later, the cigarette was snubbed out and Willie crossed the street and entered the Blue Goose.

Willie walked behind the bar and directly into the manager's office. The bartender didn't react at all since such action on Willie's part was commonplace. He didn't bother knocking on the office door upon entering. The proprietor looked up at Willie.

"Didn't expect you for another week. My extortion rates going up again?"

"Oh, come on! Extortion is such an ugly word. Call it membership dues."

"Membership in what exactly?"

"The St. Louis Chamber of Commerce."

"What do you want, Willie?"

"The sharp dressed old man, I need you to get him out of his room."

"How?"

"I don't know, tell him he has a visitor at the bar or something, stall him for a few minutes."

"Fine, I'll send someone up."

Willie disappeared to a dark, quiet corner of the bar near the stairs and waited for Charles to make his entrance. A few minutes later Charles approached the bar. The bartender offered him a complementary drink and told him the manager wanted to meet with him, a courtesy paid to all patrons.

Once outside Charles' room, Willie used his master key and let himself in. The former detective was looking for anything that would give him the upper hand in future dealings with the old man. Willie hated surprises and had no intention of committing to a job without knowing every detail beforehand.

After thoroughly searching the room from top to bottom he came up empty. The only sign that Charles even occupied the room was his suit coat hanging in the closet. The old man had traveled from God knows where and showed up to St. Louis with only the clothes on his back. He didn't bring any luggage, a briefcase, not a single file. The details of his mission were stored safely in his memory. Willie was impressed; Charles' reputation was truly deserved.

Willie felt a sharp pain in his lower back. Without even realizing what was happening, he lost all sensation in his left hip and left leg, rendering him unable to stand. Willie collapsed to the floor with a thud and stared at the ceiling. He blinked his eyes a few times and tried to gather his wits. During his tenure in law enforcement he had grown accustomed to violence, enabling him to push through the panic and center his mind on survival. Willie ignored the excruciating pain and ran his right hand down his side and reached for the pistol holstered in the small of his back.

"Mr. McCallon, on your trip to the floor I took the liberty of relieving you of your weapon. You could try for the knife you keep tucked into your boot but you should probably know you will never stand again. So do us both a favor and remain on the floor."

"You're a psychopath. You came to us to get a job done, we were going to help you and you stab me! Why? Why'd you do this? Your job, whatever the fuck it is, will never happen now!"

"Mr. McCallon, I've done more than just stab you."

Willie was starting to get light headed but fought hard to keep his mind sharp. "What did you do to me you old geezer?"

"I pierced one of your kidneys with an icepick and ruptured the L2 disc in your spine. I wasn't expecting it, but I got a happy little gift for my effort. Your L2 nerve was severed, that's why you'll never stand again. Not that it matters, you won't live to see another day."

"Just end it already, shoot me in the head and get it over with."

Charles calmly retrieved the rickety chair from the other side of the room and sat a few feet from his victim. "William, my dear man, it would be downright rude of me to deny you the answer to your question."

Willie coughed up blood and wiped his mouth with the back of his hand. "Question?"

"You had inquired about what motivated this attack. The simple answer is that I do not trust you. Your intrusion into my room helps to illustrate my point. You were a corrupt policeman and have become even more unscrupulous given that you are not accountable to anyone. I am grateful that you stopped by, William; you spared me a trip to your residence. Much simpler this way."

"Fuck you, you slimy piece of shit."

"Mr. McCallon, I normally frown on such vulgarity, but seeing as you're not long for this world, I think we can make an exception."

Willie fought through the pain. He accepted the obvious fact that Charles was right; he was not long for this world. Acceptance brought peace and calm. "You're really something, you know that? You have no issue killing someone, but an F-bomb bothers you?"

Charles looked at Willie with cold, dead eyes and smiled. "I just prefer to keeps things civilized. Vulgarity is the hallmark of an uneducated mind. I've been practicing this craft since long before you were born, Mr. McCallon, and I can tell you with great certainty that the sharpest minds I battled didn't need to rely on swearing to get their point across."

"You're done in St. Louis. All your big, fancy plans are finished."

"Oh, far from it, Mr. McCallon. Your lieutenants want you dead. Even the bartender at this fine establishment was happy to participate in your demise."

Willie rapidly blinked his eyes and looked at Charles, and then his gaze became more and more vacant.

He gasped for breath. "You … done."

"Mr. McCallon! Stay with me! We're almost finished. I need you to look at me." Charles reached forward and slapped his cheek. Charles grabbed his chin and turned his head. "I need you to look at me. There we go. I know your secret, Mr. McCallon. The one you have gone to great lengths to hide. Your partner, Frank, is more than your business associate, isn't he?"

Willie's bottom lip quivered as he closed his eyes. "Please don't."

"William, that all depends on you. The NASA engineer is here in St. Louis, isn't he?"

Willie nodded his head.

"Good. I already knew that of course, I just wanted to see if you had decided to start telling the truth for once in your life. Frank is depending on you to be honest, his life depends on it. We're off to a good start."

"I love him, please."

"I know you do, William. Wise of you to hide your relationship. Your subordinates no doubt lack a more… shall we say *enlightened* tolerance and would no doubt kill you and Frank. When I offered to dispose of you in exchange for their loyalty they jumped at the chance. However, the one thing they could not provide, the one thing you still have that I want is the engineer. So here we are."

"Why is he so important to you?"

"Mr. McCallon, please. I beg you not to venture back towards deception, you were doing so well. Only honesty will keep your dear Frank alive. You know why the engineer is important. You know exactly why. It's the reason you've kept his identity a secret for so long. Tell me where he is so I won't have to resort to more … distasteful methods of interrogation with Frank. Spare your love a painful death. Tell me where to find him and Frank will live."

"He's the bartender. The engineer is downstairs."

Realization slowly crept over the assassin's face as a faint smile could be seen. "Well, that would explain his enthusiasm to be rid of you. I suppose he thought his secret would follow you to the grave."

"The things he knows. The things he can do. In the wrong hands, very dangerous."

"I'm counting on it. Goodbye, Mr. McCallon." Charles drove the icepick into the dying man's ear. Willie flinched for a split second and was no more.

CHAPTER FOUR

"Richard, your name sounds familiar. Why is that?" Father Nathan Elias could tell that his question was making Richard Dupree nervous so he decided not to push the issue any further should the man not answer. Nathan was certain the name should mean something to him. The man sitting next to him was a stranger, he was certain he had never laid eyes on the man in his entire life. Well, he couldn't really be certain at all. Richard had dirty, matted hair down to his shoulders and a full beard. What little skin he could see on his face was caked in dirt. Give this guy a haircut, shave, and a shower and a different man could be looking back at him.

Nathan waited for an answer to the point just prior of awkward silence and realized he hadn't properly introduced himself. "Mr. Dupree, it is a pleasure to meet you. I'm Father Nathan Elias."

"Catholic?" Richard still felt the weight of holding a conversation. Every word uttered didn't feel real, like someone else had spoken it.

"Well, yes, I've never known another religious institution to use it. Can't say I'm well versed in religions outside my own. Others use Pastor, Minister, and some other titles I'm sure. Did you go to church, my son?"

Richard thought back to the very last time he had been inside a church building. The day he murdered the pedophile that had been abusing young children, his own included. *They didn't see me do anything down there.* As if masturbating under a table and hiding your erection from children made the whole thing perfectly normal. "No, Father, I haven't set foot in a church building in a great many years. I have no idea what brought me to one today."

"Yes you do, Richard, yes you do. From what little you have said so far it is quite clear that you are burdened with a guilt that is crushing you. You feel responsible for something terrible. You said you have to make things right. Why don't we start there? What is it you need to do exactly?"

Richard shifted forward in his seat and rubbed his temples. His eyes filled with tears. "Do you believe in resurrection?"

"Well, my son, the resurrection of Jesus Christ is a pretty big deal with Christians."

"I'm talking more recent, like present day."

"Someone rising from the dead? Anything is possible with the Lord."

"No offense, but lately I feel like God is on vacation and we're fending for ourselves down here."

"Don't worry about offending me, my son. We all struggle with faith. Why do you speak of resurrection? Did you lose someone dear to you?"

Richard slumped down in the pew and struggled to speak. "Yes."

"They are in a better place. You can find peace knowing they are with the Lord."

"It's not that simple. I have to make it right."

Father Elias put his hand on Richard's shoulder. "Any man seeking revenge should first dig two graves."

Richard spent a few seconds contemplating what the priest said and asked, "Is that in the bible?"

"No, my son, but wise words nonetheless."

"I dug my grave long ago, Father."

"Richard, you said earlier that all of this is your fault. That you are to blame for everything. What does that mean?"

"I could have done things differently. I sacrificed everything. Our future, our way of life." Richard's body shook violently, torment and anguish clawed at his soul. His sobs came out as screams, echoing across the walls of the church. "I lost them both! My sweet little babies! I couldn't even save my own children! I never meant for it to happen. I promise I am going to make things right. He has the answer, I want to believe." Richard collapsed into the arms of the priest, continuing to cry out in agony.

The priest wasn't sure if Richard could even hear him but spoke anyway. "Yes, Richard, Jesus not only has the answer, He is the answer."

Father Elias was prepared to sit with Richard for

however long it took. The sobbing subsided in time, followed by the heavy breathing that accompanies slumber. When the broken man began to snore, Nathan slowly and carefully laid him down in the pew and covered him up with a blanket. The priest retrieved his bible from the lectern and sat down next to Richard and began to read. If the poor man slept for ten minutes or ten hours, Nathan was not going to leave his side.

The priest awoke to the sound of horses on the street next to the church. Nathan hadn't realized he had even dozed off but was not surprised. At his age, an afternoon nap was a necessity. He looked out the window to find darkness and realized he had slept for a few hours. Nathan looked to his left to find Richard sleeping peacefully.

Father Elias quietly walked to the lobby and peered out the window. Two men were dismounting their horses. They looked to be in their mid-thirties. Both men were wearing camouflage clothes, not military uniforms, more like hunters Nathan thought. With their rifles slung to their shoulders, the two men made their way to the front door of the church. Nathan was a man of peace that welcomed anyone into his church; however, he did not welcome guns.

Nathan opened the door and stood on the landing. "Hello there, gentleman! What brings you to these parts? Doing some hunting? You'd be wise to steer clear of the east side of the river; Merle tends to shoot trespassers without so much as a word. You boys from around here?"

The two men exchanged glances that made Nathan nervous. Based on their body language, it was clear which one was giving orders and the other was following those orders. The boss nodded, apparently granting the subordinate permission to speak. "Tell me, Padre, you get any strangers lately?"

Nathan did not like being called "Padre" by a non-Spanish speaking individual. Use of the word was usually meant to mock the Catholic Church or religion in general. Nathan knew that lying was a sin but given the circumstance, the safety of his visitor could be in jeopardy. "Other than you boys, can't say that I have."

"You sure about that?" The boss glared at Nathan.

"What's this about, boys?"

The subordinate was visibly upset and looked to his boss for guidance. Bossman held up his hand to calm the other and spoke. "Show him."

A piece of paper was shoved in Nathan's hand. The priest had to look twice, but it was clear that the man in the picture was asleep on one of his pews. Richard was clean-cut in the picture. His hair was neatly trimmed and had no facial hair.

"Look real close, Padre, ever seen that man?" Bossman watched the priest closely to gauge his reaction.

"Who is he?"

"Richard Dupree, former Commanding General of the Pacific States of America."

It finally dawned on Nathan. *I knew that name sounded familiar*. "What'd he do? He in trouble?"

Bossman smiled for the first time and chuckled. "You could say that. Man's a war criminal with a price on his head."

Father Elias looked at the two men with a quizzical look. "War criminal? There isn't a functioning government in North America. Who on earth would be hunting war criminals?"

"Never said a government was looking for him. He's worth fifty pounds of silver dead, a hundred alive. We've been tracking him for months. Got him cornered in this valley, safe bet he's in this town somewhere. You wouldn't mind if we take a look inside?"

"I don't think that's necessary, I've been here all day, just me here."

Bossman brought the rifle down from his shoulder. "Step aside, Padre."

"Look here, boys. This is a house of the Lord; I won't have guns inside this church!"

"If I didn't know better, Padre, I'd think you were lying to us. But that can't be, a man of God telling a lie."

The priest's desperation was clear. "Please, I just don't want anyone to get hurt. Let me go inside and talk to him. I'm sure he'll surrender peacefully."

"Well, Padre, someone's gonna get hurt!" The bounty hunter unsheathed a knife from his belt and plunged it deep into Nathan's chest. The elderly priest crumpled to the dirt. "That's what you get for lying! You should know better, Padre! Bible thumpin' old fuck protecting a piece of shit like Dupree!"

The junior thug gurgled out a cry of pain. Bossman turned around and was sprayed in the face by a spurt of blood. He watched in horror as his partner looked to him, his eyes pleading for help. His neck was sliced open from side to side. Blood spewed from his open wound, pulsing out in jets that no doubt matched his heartbeat. The soon to be dead man hurtled towards him like he had been ejected through the windshield of a wrecked car and the two men crashed to the ground.

Richard bolted forward and kicked the rifle from Bossman's hand. Richard grabbed the hair of the corpse and rolled it to the side so he could deal with his final victim. Like a rabid animal, Richard pounded his fists into the murderer until the man gave up the struggle. Richard stood up and retrieved the rifle from a few feet away and returned. He drove the butt of the rifle down onto the bounty hunter's right hand, breaking every bone.

"I should kill you for murdering a defenseless old man, but I need you to deliver a message. You go back and tell Maxwell Harris I'm not ready to come home!"

CHAPTER FIVE

Maxwell Harris and his wife, Elizabeth, stood at the rear of the SUV looking at a frail Theodore Forrest. The dying man, despite his ailments, was smiling ear to ear. Max was in shock, his mouth wide open and his eyes as big as saucers. Elizabeth was growing more and more frustrated as the silence continued. Ever since the war ended, she felt her husband slipping further and further away from her. It was clear to her that Max was keeping a very big secret from her.

"Who's up to no good? What's he talking about, Max? What's going on?"

Theodore gave Max a surprised look as if to say *You didn't tell her?* Max was still processing the miracle revelation he had just heard and realized the cat had been let out of the bag. "Elizabeth, run and get Vanessa and James so they can see Theo."

"First tell me what's going on."

"Now is not the time, Elizabeth, Theo has spent a long time away from his wife and son. Don't make him wait any longer, please hurry."

Elizabeth knew her husband was simply trying to get rid of her but also knew he was right. For Theo's sake, she did not push the issue any further and headed to the front gate. Once she was out of earshot, Max held the hand of his friend and looked at him with compassion. "How long?"

"I should have died two weeks ago. I've been fighting it with every fiber of my being to survive long enough to see you. I imagine once I'm comfortable in my own bed, I'll go to sleep and that will be it."

"Where have you been all this time? What happened? Why didn't you get word to us that you were alive? We could have sent for you."

"It's a very long story my friend that I don't have time to tell. None of that matters, Maxwell, what matters is that I'm here now."

"Theodore, I have to know how you got like this. You were healthy when you left."

"Took an ass beating a while back, infection set in, thought I was getting better and caught pneumonia. I'm an old man and pneumonia is this world we created is a death sentence. Isaac sent some men to get some antibiotics and they were killed."

"Tell me about Isaac and his people, do you trust them?"

"I do, completely. And you're going to trust them when I'm gone. You will need them for what's next."

"But you didn't trust Isaac enough to tell him what you just told me."

"Trust wasn't the reason I kept him out of the loop. I simply wanted the first person to hear the news be you and you alone. You deserve as much."

"Start from the beginning, tell me everything."

"When I left here with my team we had one mission – find Dupree at all costs. I was prepared to go to the gates of hell to bring him back here to you."

"I had it on good authority that he killed all of you."

"I'm the only one that survived. I never thought one man could be a match against two dozen men. The things he did, Maxwell, he's nothing more than a psychopath. He slaughtered us … we never had a chance. He got us to split up and took us out two or three at a time until it was just me. Do you know why he did that?"

"He's done it many times to taunt me, you weren't the first."

"Son of a bitch kept me alive to tell you …"

"That he's not ready to come home yet, yes, I know, I've heard it many times. After what he did the bastard has the nerve to think this is his home."

"I thought the same thing but turns out we're both wrong. He knows this isn't his home."

"So what the hell is he talking about, Theo?"

Theo began gasping for air and started wheezing violently. This made Max nervous. Theo produced a canteen and sipped some water. Theo tried his best to calm Max. "It's okay, I'm fine, really."

"Are you sure? We still have some medical staff

here."

"No, it's okay."

"You were saying about his home?"

"Yes, he knows his home is not here. I knew he would probably end up killing me if he caught me, I knew I couldn't stop him but I had to at least keep tabs on him in the hopes some crazy opportunity presented itself."

"Where'd he go?"

"He went to Beck Estates, or what's left of it."

"He went to Beck Estates? You're serious? Why?"

Theo was quickly losing his strength and began to whisper. "He found something."

"We searched every square inch of Beck Estates when the power grid went down for good. Howard's lab had a lot of what we needed and we took all of it. Nothing of value left."

"There's more. He was talking to someone."

"Who?"

"No idea. He was alone. But it wasn't like when you're alone and you talk to yourself. You might catch yourself saying something out loud like 'Well, this is a fine mess you got yourself into' but it was more than that. It was like listening to one side of a conversation."

"Maybe he was talking to the memory of Howard." Max had to remind himself that Richard had just as much right to the memory of Howard Beck as he did. Richard was there when he died and the last words spoken by the most brilliant mind of the twenty-first century were spoken to Richard Dupree.

"No, that wasn't it. Dupree wasn't being sentimental or nostalgic; he was driven by some purpose."

Max shot his old friend a mischievous grin. "For a man on death's door, you'd think you'd get to the point."

"Hey, you said to tell you everything."

"My wife will be here soon with your family."

"I'm surprised at you, Maxwell. You mean your wife will be here soon. Why on earth are keeping this from her?"

Max was wounded by such a blunt question. "I

have my reasons."

As if on cue, Vanessa and James Forrest came sprinting down the path to the SUV. Wife and son exchanged tearful hugs with the patriarch back from the grave. Isaac Lynwood had four of his men move Theo to a gurney and the dying man was moved into the compound to rest one last time in his own bed.

Elizabeth Harris stared directly at her husband, waiting patiently for an explanation. Max looked at her briefly and walked toward the front gate. Elizabeth followed. "What's was Theo talking about? Who's up to no good? Who are you supposed to stop?"

"I don't know. Theo didn't get a chance to tell me."

"Bullshit! I saw the look on your face; you knew exactly what he was talking about. Maxwell Harris, you better start talking or so help me …"

"Or what? You'll do what, Elizabeth? Stop letting me fuck you like you always do when you want your way? You've always treated sex like a weapon, so trust me, sweetheart, I'm used to it."

"Oh, please! You're too much of a drunk to even get it up, so gimme a break." Max ignored her and kept walking. "That's right, Max, just ignore the problem and it'll go away. You're a pathetic drunk with a permanent case of whiskey dick!" Elizabeth made sure to speak up towards the end to humiliate her husband.

Max gritted his teeth and kept walking. His wife was more proficient in verbal judo than he was and she had no problem airing their dirty laundry in front of everyone. He felt terrible for what he said to her but had no intention of apologizing. He'd rather have another reason to hate himself. Max could never bring himself to commit suicide, so he would spend the rest of his life punishing himself for making the wrong decision on that day four years ago.

The Forrest residence was similar to the others in the compound. The RV-Towns that sprouted up prior to the collapse were still prevalent over a decade later. The difference now was that the RV-Towns had become fortified and the once mobile homes had planted roots. Max knocked on the door and waited. Theo's son opened the door, nodded, and disappeared to the rear of the RV. Max stepped inside and sat down. Thirty minutes passed, then an hour. Vanessa stepped from the rear compartment and slid the door behind her. Max stood to greet her.

"Vanessa, I …"

Vanessa Forrest slapped Max as hard as she could across the face. Max just stood there in complete shock, his cheek red and stinging. Mrs. Forrest was one of the kindest, gentlest people he had ever known. Not once had he witnessed her losing her temper.

"You son of a bitch. You told me he was dead. You told me he died over a year ago!"

"Vanessa, I'm sorry. I'm just as shocked as you are. I don't know how this happened."

"Just when I finally accepted that my husband was gone, just when I started to fall in love again. I've been having sex with another man in the same bed my husband is going to die in! Do you have any idea how ashamed I feel right now?"

Max could barely stand to hear himself speak. "Do you want me to leave?"

"Yes, very much so. But he's asking for you. Have my son come get me when you leave." Vanessa stormed out the door and slammed it behind her.

Max stood perfectly still and stared at the bedroom door. He tried to will himself to move forward but found himself frozen in place. He knew he had no choice but confront the nightmare he created. The thought of Theo cutting him in two with a shotgun felt like a fitting end to his miserable existence so he moved forward.

"Max? Max? Are you out there?"

"Uh, yeah."

"Well get in here."

Max slid the door open and stepped in. *Damn, no shotgun.* "Theo, I'm sorry. You don't deserve this."

"I deserve to see my wife and son before I go, and I did. The rest doesn't matter. She feels guilty but I keep telling her it's okay. She didn't know. I want her to be happy after I'm gone and in time she'll forgive herself. She needs someone to blame and you're the most qualified it seems. Give her time, she'll get over it."

"Again, I'm sorry."

"Stop it. We don't have much time and I want my family here for the end."

"Okay."

"What was the last thing I told you?"

"Beck Estates."

"Ah, yes. He found something. I don't know what, but he found something. Knew exactly where it was. This invisible person he was talking to seemed to be leading him right to it."

"Where was it?"

"In what was left of the library."

"The library? He didn't go to the lab?"

"No, straight to the library and straight out."

"Ghost of Howard need to do some reading?"

"Dupree's crazy enough to think it."

"Wait, how did you get close enough to see him go into the library and live to tell about it?"

"I thought I told you."

"No, you didn't."

"I can see how you'd be confused. Let me put it in perspective. I was hiding at least three hundred yards away. Right before he walked in the main entrance, he stopped, stood there a few seconds like he was making up his mind, then he turned around and called out to me."

"What?"

"Yeah, thought I was dead for sure. He called out my name and said he wanted me to join him. Promised he wouldn't kill me, kept saying it was okay. I don't know why, but I believed him. He was as giddy as a schoolboy, never seen him act like that."

"He really has gone insane."

"Well, no way I was getting near him. Kept my distance. By the time I got to the doorway I saw him running out of the library laughing like a madman. Told me had finally had the key to put an end to everything.

Wanted me to tell you that you'd be sorry. Sorry for what, Maxwell?"

"That I didn't shoot him in the head the last time we saw each other."

CHAPTER SIX

The elderly assassin was no stranger to clean up. He'd disposed of many bodies over the previous decades. Many were done in haste; others were done in the same casual manner that one would spend doing the dishes after a large meal. Regardless of the timeline, all had been done with an efficiency that guaranteed Charles would not be pursued by either the authorities or interested parties seeking revenge. The world Charles operated in no longer had a criminal justice system that demanded prosecution for his crimes so that concern didn't cross his mind. Had he not planned for every contingency, Charles would have been concerned that the dead man's partner and lover, Frank, would find out about Willie's demise and come after him. The assassin never left the slightest detail up to chance. Frank would be disposed of before he knew what had happened to Willie. Charles would deal with the final loose end in short time.

Any rational person standing over their own murder victim would be alarmed by a knock at the door. Charles was not. He was not expecting a visitor but was not surprised by one either. The old man took a handkerchief from his pocket and cleaned Willie's blood from his hands and forearms. The odds of having to defend himself from the person behind the door were quite low in Charles' assessment, but as always, every contingency must be planned for.

The door was cracked ever so slightly. The bartender was standing in the hall. He looked over Charles' shoulder and saw Willie on the floor. "Holy shit, you really killed him, I can't believe it."

"Let's not discuss this in the hall. Please, come in."

The bartender took a few steps into the room and looked at the body. He gasped and brought his hand to his mouth. "That's so disgusting."

"I envy you, sir; I've been doing this far too long. This sort of thing does not bother me in the slightest."

The bartender was disturbed by the old man's

honesty. Only a psychopath could stab someone to death and feel nothing. Such a statement made him fear for his own safety. He nervously looked toward the door and thought about darting out.

"Relax, Mr. Curry."

"What? I'm, uh, I'm fine."

"You were just thinking that I might decide to kill you."

"Me? Naw, I wasn't thinking that."

"Yes you were. I wouldn't be proficient in my line of work if I couldn't read human behavior. It's really quite easy, anyone can do it. All one has to do is pay attention to the little things. The human body will always betray what the mind is thinking. I've become so talented at it I find most people can be read like a book."

The bartender laughed nervously, hoping to ease the tension. "You must make a fortune playing poker."

"Let's just say I prefer the stakes to be much higher than money. More fun that way. You ever play a game with stakes that high?" The smile left Charles' face and he glared at the bartender with malice.

The tension in the room was not eased in the slightest. The bartender was now certain he would join Willie on the floor. Charles pursed his lips and locked eyes with Mr. Curry. The assassin found that direct confrontation resulted in a man's true colors. His intelligence, character, bravery, and his temperament could be sized up in mere seconds.

Charles grinned from ear to ear and laughed. "Mr. Curry, you really do need to relax! If you can't find humor in a brutal murder you haven't lived! I know you hated this man, celebrate! Spit on his corpse or something. Have some fun."

The bartender finally knew this madman wasn't going to kill him but still found the enthusiastic charm he exuded very disturbing. If the two men weren't in the same room as a dead body, he could easily think that Charles was an evangelical preacher trying to bring him the good Word.

"Mr. Curry, I'm afraid I'm going to have to ask a

favor of you."

The bartender knew he couldn't refuse and dreaded the question. "What do you need?"

"Oh, before we get to that, I don't believe I know your first name."

"Sebastian."

"Sebastian! What a unique name, I positively love it. Family name?"

"Uh, no. My mother loved Bach."

"I guess she didn't favor the name Johann."

Sebastian couldn't take his eyes from the dead body. Willie seemed to be staring directly at him. "You needed a favor?"

"Yes, shouldn't prove too difficult. I simply need you to lock this room and remain in the hallway until I return."

"You're leaving?"

"I'm afraid so. I have a small matter that needs tending to. While Mr. McCallon's sudden departure proved a convenient gift, it has put me slightly ahead of schedule and I need to call on some of my colleagues. I won't be long. When I return I shall dispose of Mr. McCallon. I also look forward to discussing your future."

Sebastian felt like he heard an odd inflection on the word 'future.' He finally took his eyes from the corpse and looked at Charles. "My future? What do you mean?"

Charles smiled and paused a beat, studying Sebastian. *The human body will always betray what the mind is thinking.* "Why this fine establishment of course! Now that Mr. McCallon will be unable to collect his fifty percent I imagine you have big plans in store. Am I right?"

"Wh- why do you care? You gonna take his fifty percent?"

"No, no, no, Mr. Curry. I wouldn't dream of it! I have nothing but the utmost respect for a man that makes an honest living by the sweat of his brow. Besides, I'm not a fan of St. Louis, no offense."

"None taken."

"Good. I just want the opportunity to propose a business venture to you. An investment in the future if you will."

"Uh, sure. I guess we can talk when you get back." Sebastian had wished he'd never agreed to help this lunatic. Getting rid of Willie McCallon was too good to pass up. Scores of people would celebrate his death and even piss on his grave. After five minutes alone with Charles, he was actually starting to miss Willie.

"Excellent, Mr. Curry. I'll be back within the hour. Thank you for your help."

Sebastian simply nodded his head and watched Willie's murderer stroll down the hall like it was just another day at the office heading for his lunch break. Sebastian thought back to the violence of the previous decade he had gone to great lengths to avoid at all costs. Some would call Sebastian a coward, Sebastian considered himself smarter with a very strong sense of self-preservation. He was a man of science and his mind was his only weapon. And since his mind had not attained superhero powers that could stop vicious beatings, avoiding conflict and often hauling ass in the other direction was the most logical solution.

Sebastian stood in the deserted hallway for what seemed like an eternity before Charles returned. The bartender felt terrified under the steely gaze of assassin. Sebastian simply stared back at Charles not having a clue if he should be doing something. Charles enjoyed making the man uncomfortable.

"Mr. Curry?"

"Uh, yeah?"

"Would you please open the door?"

"Oh, yeah, hold on." Sebastian fumbled in his pockets for the key and opened the door. He stood back and allowed Charles to step in and followed him. Once they were inside, Sebastian locked the door.

"Do you have a laundry cart, Mr. Curry?"

"I changed the sheets in here myself."

"I'm not concerned about fresh linen, Mr. Curry; I mean to dispose of the dearly departed Mr. McCallon."

"Got it, sure, we got a laundry cart. I'll go get it."

"Not so fast, Mr. Curry. Mr. McCallon isn't going anywhere. Besides, my plan is to wait until nightfall to move the body. The laundry cart can wait for now. I just wanted to ensure that you had one just in case I had to make other arrangements. I've been very eager to chat with you, Dr. Biggs."

Sebastian felt his heart leap up into his throat. He did his best to remain calm. He tried to think fast and come up with something to say but all he could manage was a confused look.

"I know who you are, doctor."

"I'm not a doctor. Just a bartender. Wouldn't be a very good one, can't stand the sight of blood." The bartender looked down at the bloody remains of Willie McCallon and grimaced, followed by a goofy smile that said *see what I mean? Yuck!*

Charles smiled and sat down in the rickety chair next to the corpse. He motioned for Sebastian to sit down on the bed, which he did. "Sebastian, you can relax, no need to maintain this charade any longer. I know you're not a medical doctor; I was referring to the two doctorates that grant you the title. You received your first Ph.D. in astrophysics from Harvard and your second in artificial intelligence from MIT which makes you the most educated bartender in the world." Charles laughed at his clever joke but all he got in return from Dr. Biggs was a look of horror. "In your first year at MIT you met Howard Beck, aged fifteen. The young lad was infatuated with your fiancé, wasn't he? He insisted that you end the relationship because he was convinced he was going to marry your bride to be, which he eventually did some years later. You remained close friends with Meredith Beck and eventually become a co-founder of Beck Enterprises. I can assume that since you held the position of chief operating officer of Beck Enterprises for as long as you did that you were one of the few people Howard could tolerate. I might even venture a brave guess that the two of you were very close friends. Tell me, how did Howard take it when you left to head up NASA?"

Sebastian decided the best course of action was to remain silent and not make matters worse.

"I must say, Dr. Biggs, I've been looking for you for a very long time. Simon Sterling was convinced you were dead, but I was determined not to give up on you until I had proof. I had no idea when we first met that you were the man I was looking for. The only photograph I have of you is close to fifteen years old. Your plastic surgeon did some wonderful work. If Mr. McCallon hadn't revealed your identity I would've never figured it out."

Sebastian tried his best to maintain a stone cold poker face but found it difficult given that he could feel himself starting to hyperventilate. Sprinting out of the room felt like the natural course of action but he knew Charles would probably break his kneecaps. Keeping his mouth shut for the time being still seemed prudent.

"I've been looking forward to this day for so long, Doctor. It truly is an honor to finally meet you." Charles smiled and paused a beat to allow Sebastian to speak. "Come now, Doctor, cat got your tongue?"

"I told you, I'm not a doctor. My name is Sebastian Curry."

"I've had plastic surgery myself, more than once, actually. And for the same reason that you had yours, to shed one identity and slip into another. There is one thing that even the most skilled surgeon can never change – the eyes. Sure you can put on contacts and change your eye color, but there's something about the eyes, something singular and unique. I look deep into yours and I know *exactly* who I see looking back at me." Charles dropped his pleasant demeanor and looked sternly at Sebastian. "Doctor, let's not waste any more time playing this game."

"What do you want?"

Charles relaxed and leaned back in his seat. "Is it true that you were there when Howard brought Hal online for the first time?"

Sebastian had hoped this day would never come, but he couldn't deny its arrival. "No, Howard did his best work alone. He preferred to be free from distraction."

"I thought as much. Funny how history is rewritten, don't you think?"

"Howard's wife and I were the first people that Howard introduced to Hal. Truth be told, Hal was online for weeks before Howard let us meet him. The more accurate version of events wasn't exciting enough I guess."

"One of the most historic events in all of mankind's brief existence and you were there. I envy you, sir."

"I hate to tell you, but you've come a long way and wasted many years finding me. Hal is gone. Nothing will bring him back. Howard should have never entrusted Hal's care to Richard Dupree."

"Dr. Biggs, your expertise in artificial intelligence is not the reason I sought you out. Seeing as how you were the last man to head up NASA, I'm hoping you can help me get into space."

CHAPTER SEVEN

Death was Richard Dupree's constant companion. No matter how hard he tried to keep death at bay, the people he came into contact with inevitably suffered a violent death. For this reason, he had spent the previous four years in seclusion. On rare occasions when he had to come into contact with people, he ended up either killing someone or getting someone killed. Today was no different. He felt no remorse for the bounty hunter he had killed. That man's blood was on Maxwell Harris for sending him in the first place. Richard did, however, feel a great deal of remorse over the death of Father Elias. The elderly priest had dedicated his life to helping others with no expectation of earthly reward. The old man gave his life attempting to protect Richard and that troubled Richard a great deal.

The ex-Navy SEAL had a fierce sense of self-preservation and his instincts told him to move on and put as much distance as he could from this tragic ordeal. Death was almost always followed by consequence. Few people left this world without affecting the living, family and friends are left to deal with the aftermath. Some grieve and move on; others have their lives torn apart and never find a way to pick up the pieces. The ones that Richard Dupree were concerned with were those seeking vengeance. Brutal murder attracts vengeance in some form or another. While he did not personally take Father Elias' life, those seeking retribution would not be bothered by the truth. They would blame Richard nonetheless. While Richard felt guilt over the man's death, he did not feel guilty enough to pay with his own life. This simple reality screamed at Richard to get the hell out of there and not look back but he just could not bring himself to leave Father Elias above ground to rot in the sun. The man deserved better.

Richard turned around and looked to the hillside to see how much time he had to bury the priest. He knew he had already wasted far too much time agonizing over what had happened and now he had a decision to make.

At the bottom of the hill a few hundred yards away he spotted a row of houses. In front of one of the houses was a little boy staring back at him. Richard judged the boy to be maybe seven or eight and wondered if he witnessed the attack. The child didn't appear to be upset or afraid, only curious at the sight of a filthy looking hobo at the top of the hill outside the church.

If he keeps playing I have time. Richard willed the little boy to pick up the ball at his feet or get on his bicycle a few feet away. He did neither and remained in place looking directly at Richard. *Come on, kid, nothing to see here, hop on your bike and ride away.* The child just stood there looking at him. Richard knew he had to do something so he put on a big smile and waved. A look of terror washed over the boy and he began to cry. He turned around and ran towards the house screaming.

Adrenaline surged and Richard fought the primal instinct to run in the opposite direction. He had to make a decision before a curious father headed his way to investigate. Richard looked back towards the church and saw the dead bounty hunter's horse tied to a tree branch. He entertained the idea of securing the body behind the saddle and riding off. Once he was far enough away, he could give Father Elias a proper burial.

The plan quickly faded as he saw the boy's father emerge from the house with a baseball bat. The man saw Richard and started jogging up the hill. Richard looked at the fresh blood on his hands courtesy of the beating he delivered to the bounty hunter and knew things were about to go south in a hurry.

"You there! Get your filthy ass out of here! No one wants you here! We don't give handouts to bums so get the hell out of here before I beat your ass!" The man looked to be in his early thirties and the ravages of malnutrition had taken its toll on his health. It was obvious he went without so his son could eat. Richard could tell he was all bark. It was clear that he was hoping the baseball bat would be enough to scare Richard away without confrontation.

"Look, mister, I don't want any trouble. Just take

it easy and listen to me. Something terrible just happened and I need your help."

The man raised the bat to shoulder level. "What happened? You got about two seconds to explain the blood on your hands or I'm gonna start swingin'."

"About ten minutes ago I was in the church talking to Father Elias when this crazy guy showed up. He stabbed him to death before I could kill him. I tried to stop it, he was gonna kill me too so I had no choice."

"What'd you say? Someone got stabbed to death?"

"That's what I said. Right over there." Richard pointed through the tall grass at the bodies. "That man killed Father Elias before I could kill him."

The man took his eyes off Richard for the first time and looked at the carnage ten feet away. "Fuck! Oh, Jesus, no! You're an animal!" The man started towards Richard with the bat cocked behind his head. He nervously took a few steps and hesitated before swinging, hoping Richard would start running. The hesitation only served as an obvious telegraph as to what was about to happen. Even if the man came at him full speed, Richard wouldn't have had any trouble disarming him. Richard thrust both hands forward and latched onto the man's wrists and twisted the bat free.

"Stop! I don't want to hurt you! I'm telling you the truth! It happened just like I said!"

The man dropped to his knees and raised his arms to protect his head. "I'm sorry! Please! I'm sorry! I didn't mean it! Don't hurt me!"

"Stand up, come on, get up." Richard let the bat fall to the ground. "I'm not gonna hurt you."

Richard heard the telltale sound of a shotgun racking a shell into the chamber. He froze in place and slowly raised his bloody hands.

"Good thing you done dropped the bat. Try anything I'll cut you in half. Got it?"

Richard knew better than to turn around and kept his hands up. "I know how this looks. This isn't what you think. Can I turn around and talk to you?"

"No. You're fine right where you are."

"Look, you have to let me explain. This isn't what it looks like."

"It looks like a drifter rolled into town and trouble followed him." A set of handcuffs were tossed. "Danny, you stupid fuck, why'd you come up here by yourself? Put those cuffs on him."

"Shut up, Virgil! How was I supposed to know what happened? My boy said he saw a bum wanderin' 'round and I come up here to chase him off."

"Whatever. Hey, drifter, get on your stomach and put your hands in the small of your back. Stand up, you die."

"I'll do whatever you say, just take it easy. Will I have a chance to explain myself?" Richard slowly went down to his knees and then lay on his stomach.

"Oh you're gonna have plenty of time to explain things to the judge."

Danny picked up the baseball bat and slammed it down hard on Richard's buttocks. "Stay your nasty ass on the ground, you hear me?" Danny placed the handcuffs on Richard's wrists.

Richard laughed. "Judge? You boys got a judge?"

Virgil kicked dirt in Richard's face. "Damn right we got a judge. Five local towns in these parts formed a militia to protect ours. Been goin' strong for a year now. Judge'll be right proud we bagged us two vagrants before supper. Once he's done with you you'll actually do some honest work for a change. He puts bums like you to work. I hear they're working on putting up walls around our fine cities to keep trash like you out."

Richard spat dirt out of his mouth. "Two?"

"Ain't you listenin', drifter? I done said the militia's protectin' five towns, not two."

"You said two vagrants."

"Yeah, first one's the reason I come up here. One of his hands all broke up. Said he and his friend were at the church prayin' when a crazy lookin' hobo come in all psycho. Said the guy up and stabbed the priest to death and slit his friend's throat wide open. Said the guy smashed his hand so he couldn't pray no more and let him go. Now I ain't no detective but this all looks like everything he described. Watcha say, Danny? Sound about right?"

"Sure looks like it. But this one said pretty much the same thing about the dead guy over there. Said he was the one did the killin'."

This is what I get for trying to do the right thing. Should have hauled ass out of here. "The guy with the broken hand is lying his ass off. *I* was in the church with Father Elias and *they* came in looking for trouble. They killed the priest for no reason and wanted to kill me. I have every right to defend myself."

"Save it for the judge, drifter, I don't give a shit. Time to go, get up."

***

While Richard had spent the previous four years in seclusion, he did, however, maintain constant surveillance of what was left of the former United States. Whenever he moved from one place to the other, he made it a point to observe, from a distance, the nearby towns along the way to better prepare himself should trouble follow him, which it often did. With the Pacific States of America and the Unified American Empire relics of the past thanks to the Chinese War, a nationwide or even statewide government could not be found anywhere. It was common to see fortified towns with armed patrols and secured gates monitoring entry. The once great nation had reverted to a vast collection of medieval castles.

In all his time wandering about, Richard had never seen anything close to a collection of scattered towns banding together to form a militia and pulling it off with any degree of success. Such an endeavor required an infrastructure and government of sorts, a small group of people telling a larger group of people what to do. Much like the nationwide government that had collapsed eleven years prior, any time two or more towns tried to band together, corruption and violence led to their downfall. Richard was both curious and terrified to see how these hillbillies managed to keep it together for a year.

"When's the last time you washed your nasty ass or put on fresh clothes?" Virgil sat atop his horse pulling Richard along behind him by a rope.

"Don't know, not planning on it anytime soon."

"That's disgusting, the fuck is wrong with you?"

"People tend to steer clear of you when you look like I do."

"Folks might also be inclined to think you's a crazy person goin' 'round killin' people."

"Folks like this judge of yours?"

"I ain't gonna lie to you, drifter, things ain't lookin' to go your way."

Richard was not delusional enough to think this "judge" would care to hear his side of the story. Once the bounty hunter produced the wanted poster to the judge and revealed Richard's war criminal status, the chances of Richard regaining his freedom would be a challenge.

Time to start planning my escape. "What happened with the guy with the broken hand? You find him or did he come to you?"

"Enough talkin', crazy man. Shut up."

"I just wanna know what lies he told you."

"I said shut up! I ain't your friend, you fuckin' scumbag. One more word and this horse is gonna end up draggin' your ass the rest of the way!"

Richard had endured all manner of physical abuse in his days but being dragged by a horse was not one of them so he took the warning seriously. The most crucial thing he could deduce at that point was that the bounty hunter had kept his identity a secret. The most likely reason was greed – he didn't want to share the bounty with anyone unless it was absolutely necessary.

The two men walked for another thirty minutes and arrived at what used to be a large gas station. The pumps had long since been removed and the building had been fortified with iron bars and sandbags. Virgil dismounted his horse and leveled his shotgun at Richard's chest.

"Get on inside. Walk slow and don't do nothin'

stupid. Get within ten feet of me and you die. Got it?"

"Yeah."

"Morgan! Get your ass out here, boy! Got us a prisoner!"

Richard slowly walked towards the entrance and was greeted by a stocky man in his late twenties. Richard had the amusing thought that they had arrived at a nightclub and this guy was the bouncer. Morgan eyed Richard. "You are one nasty lookin' sumbitch. We gonna have any problems outta you, boy?"

"I'd like a room with a king sized bed and make sure the mini-bar is fully stocked. You take credit cards? I don't have any cash on me. After I get settled in send your sister up to my room."

Morgan laughed. "I like this guy! Where'd you find him?"

"Like you don't know," said Virgil.

"Come on, funny man, the penthouse suite is ready for you. I'm sure you're gonna love it." Morgan put a firm hand on Richard's elbow and led him inside. All of the shelving and merchandise had been cleared out long ago to make room for desks and storage lockers. At the center of the main room where the cash registers had once been now resembled a judge's bench from a courtroom. Richard counted six people walking around and was bothered that not one of them would look at him. It was as though they were deliberately ignoring him.

The walk-in freezer had been remodeled into an impressive holding cell. Richard was shoved inside. Morgan said, "Get some rest, funny man. Your friend there tried to bargain with the judge, wanted to split the reward money they got out on you fifty-fifty. Judge didn't quite see it that way. Figured we could handle a war criminal ourselves and collect the bounty. What the hell'd you do?"

Richard said nothing.

"Fine, don't say anything. I think it's a load of shit, no way you was some big time general." The door was slammed shut followed by the clicking of locks.

Richard turned and looked at his cellmate. The

broken hand he had given the bounty hunter was now the least of his problems. The pool of blood under his head gave Richard serious doubts as to how he was going to escape. Suddenly his odds didn't seem so good.

CHAPTER EIGHT

Maxwell Harris was tired of funerals. Long ago he had given up on developing close relationships with new people. He'd grown to respect a handful of people he had met in the last ten years, but the number of people he truly valued as a close friend was in the single digits. Theodore Forrest had taken the top spot once occupied by Richard Dupree. When the traitor pissed on the memory of Howard Beck and ran off like a coward, Theodore Forrest insisted on being the one to hunt Dupree to the ends of the earth and bring him back to answer for his crimes.

What pained Max the most was that he was now presiding over the second funeral of his dear friend. When Dupree wiped out Theo's squad over a year ago and his dear friend was presumed dead, Max had held a memorial service for the honored fallen. Now, for the second time, he had to stare out at the faces of the people that looked to him for strength and help them try to make sense of it all.

"I'm sorry. That's about all that I come up with. It's really the only thing that can sum up what I'm feeling. I made a mistake by telling all of you that Theo was gone." Max couldn't help but look into the eyes of Theo's widow. "We've all spent the past year coping with this grief in our own way and now all of that is for nothing. We have no choice but to start the process again and for that I'm sorry. I should have done better. I shouldn't have made an assumption about something as important as a man's life."

Max continued to look at Vanessa Forrest hoping to see a glimmer of anything. Forgiveness was nowhere on the list. He was holding out for acceptance or even understanding but her stern countenance didn't falter. *She needs someone to blame and you're the most qualified it seems. Give her time; she'll get over it.* Max hung his head and looked to Theodore's son to take his place at the podium so he could properly eulogize his father.

Max could feel that the widow Forrest had

extended as much of her courtesy to his presence as she could muster so Max bowed out and quietly blended his way to the back of the crowd and stood next to his wife.

Elizabeth leaned in and whispered. "What was Theo doing out there?"

"Jesus, Elizabeth! Can we put the man in the ground first?"

"So when he's in the ground you'll stop lying to me and everyone? Is that what you're saying?"

"I can't believe you're doing this now."

"Part of me hoped you'd finally come clean when you were at the podium just now, but I'm not surprised you decided to stick with the lying coward routine. It suits both of you."

"Leave Theo out of this!" Everyone within ten feet of the arguing couple looked at them in disgust.

"Do you really think anyone believed the bullshit cover-up story you and Theo dreamed up? Out of nowhere you decide to send Theo on a diplomatic assignment to Florida and on his way back his entire delegation gets ambushed and murdered by outlaws?"

"Richard Dupree is alive."

Elizabeth Harris had been lied to for over a year and no matter what, her husband had always stuck to the same lie. No matter how many holes she punched in his bullshit story he never wavered from the diplomatic fantasy he and Theo dreamed up. For one of the first times in her marriage, her husband had left her speechless. No witty comeback, no opinion to share, only stunned silence.

Max felt a huge weight lift from his shoulders. He couldn't remember the last time he felt this level of peace. More surprising, he actually smiled. "Theo was surprised I hadn't told you."

Elizabeth was overcome with a torrent of emotions. She felt joy for crossing the chasm separating her from her husband. She understood her husband's deceit came from a place of love and protection. Her fury and hatred for Richard Dupree would have led to her demise long ago if she knew the truth. Had she known

Theo's true mission, nothing would have stopped her from leaving with him to hunt down the traitor. Her husband's declining physical state prevented him from sprinting more than ten yards so Dupree was well outside his grasp. Maxwell knew the truth would take her from him so the only way to keep her safely by his side was to lie to her.

Elizabeth reached down and squeezed her husband's hand. At her touch tears welled up in his eyes. "Please don't leave, Elizabeth. Trust that I have a plan. We've sacrificed too much and we're very close to catching him."

"How many?"

"He's killed forty-seven of our people. No telling how many more that got in his way."

"Are you counting Hal?"

"Of course I'm counting Hal. He's at the top of the list. Theo's the most recent addition."

"All this time I thought when he destroyed Hal that son of a bitch died along with him."

Max paused and contemplated if it was time for the whole truth. He figured the bombshell he just dropped would take time to process. He would tell her everything soon enough. However, as always, his wife could read him like a book. "Max? What is it, sweetheart?"

Max looked into his wife's beautiful blue eyes and smiled. "Now is not the time, my dear. We need to say goodbye to our friend. This day is about him, not Richard Dupree."

Elizabeth Harris felt a renewed sense of trust in her husband and kissed his cheek.

***

After the funeral Elizabeth returned home to prepare dinner. Max still had a job to do. The day-to-day operations of a secured compound never ceased, not even for a funeral. The command center was operated out of two shipping containers laid side by side with doors cut into the walls to connect the two structures. Solar panels lined the top of the command center. Secured to the side of the command center stood a hundred foot antenna for a shortwave radio.

These days Max could find very few things he took pride in and the command center was at the top of the list. Having spent decades in chronic pain from a spinal column that would give a chiropractor nightmares, Max could not venture far from the compound. His command center was among three of the most advanced communication centers west of the Mississippi so Max had little need to travel. Five command centers were operating east of the Mississippi. The only thing the eight command centers had in common was that they possessed powerful shortwave radio transmitters that could broadcast across the continent. Anyone with the proper resources could join the club.

Every command center adopted their call sign from the nearest city that showed up on the most rudimentary maps of the former United States. The command center in front of Max was actually on the shores of Jackson Lake but derived its name from the city of Denver, some sixty miles to the southwest.

Max entered the command center and retrieved the paperwork from his tray and pretended to read them while he scanned the faces of his staff for signs of anger or resentment. Since most of his waking hours were spent navigating various stages of inebriation he never knew from day to day which people he had offended or humiliated. No one seemed to be seething in anger so Max felt safe for the time being. Max asked the room. "Anything to report?"

"Things are shaking up in St. Louis," said one of the two men sitting at the comm desk.

Max was intrigued. St. Louis had been stable for years. "Really?"

"Repeated broadcasts claim that Willie McCallon is dead."

"Son of a bitch. What the hell happened?"

"Someone killed him and his lieutenants. At least

that's what the broadcast is saying. Might be bullshit."

"How long have they been broadcasting this?"

"Little over twelve hours."

"Twelve hours is a long time to broadcast bullshit. Who's claiming power now?"

"You would think one of McCallon's rivals would be loud and proud. Whoever's running St. Louis now hasn't announced a coming out party."

"Keep me posted."

"Yes, sir."

"What else?"

"Knoxville has a report for you."

Max shuffled through the papers in his hands. "I don't see it."

"He wants to speak to you directly. He contacted us during the funeral. Offered his condolences and said he'd be available for the rest of the day."

"Far be it from me to ignore the likes of Benjamin Black. Let's get him on the horn."

"You got it." The technician flipped some switches and tweaked the dial to Knoxville's frequency. "Knoxville station, Knoxville station, this is Denver. Come in, Knoxville."

"Go ahead, Denver, this is Knoxville station."

"I have Mr. Harris on the line for Mr. Black."

"Roger, wait one."

A minute later, the booming voice of Benjamin Black filled the room. "Max? You there?"

"I'm here Ben."

"Sorry to hear about Theo. He was a good man. Give Vanessa my love."

"Will do. What's going on Ben?"

"Have some good news for you."

"We can use it."

"Your friend is coming for a visit. Should be here day after tomorrow."

Max immediately understood why his good friend wanted to deliver the news himself. "You sure he'll make it to the party this time?" Dupree had been caught before but always managed to escape custody.

"I have a welcoming committee heading straight to him. The kind folks escorting him seem to know what they're doing and have been acquainted with his talents. My people should meet up with him this time tomorrow."

"That's great news, Ben. What do you need from me?"

"Just meet me half way and he's all yours. I'll be coming along to keep him company."

"When you confirm he's in Knoxville, I'll have my people on the road. You have enough fuel?"

"You know I do, been saving up just for this."

"That great, Ben. You guys know about St. Louis?"

"Yeah, not sure what to make of it. McCallon may have been an asshole, but he kept St. Louis locked down tight for years."

"You guys know who's calling the shots now?"

"No, but I'm gonna find out. Not much choice."

"Still no way around St. Louis?"

"Afraid not. After McCallon took out the bridges in Memphis, you got two options to get a vehicle across the Mississippi – St. Louis or New Orleans."

"Is New Orleans still standing?"

"Shit, Maxwell, you know as well as I do – anyone that makes it to New Orleans is never heard from again."

"Ben, I can't let you have all the fun. Make camp a safe distance from St. Louis and wait for me to get to my side. I'll meet your recon team in the city follow them back to you. We combine our forces and cross the Mississippi together."

"Are you saying you're actually making the trip yourself?"

"You know I am. This is too important."

"What will your lovely wife say?"

"Brother, you let me worry about that."

"Fair enough. Stay close to the radio this time tomorrow. The minute our guest is comfortable I'll call you."

"I look forward to it."

***

"Honey, I'm sorry for everything."

Max and Elizabeth had retired to their bed for the evening. Patience was not Elizabeth's strong suit, but she knew that her husband was waiting for complete privacy from his walkie-talkie, from knocks on the door, from everything.

"It's okay, I promise. I understand why you kept it a secret. Everyone was better off thinking he was dead. I've slept a lot better thinking he was rotting in hell. I can't imagine the torture you've been living all this time."

"Gives my alcoholism a certain level of validation, doesn't it?"

"Where is he, Maxwell?"

"In custody on his way to Ben."

"Are you serious? He's been caught? Max, that's great news!"

"He's been caught before. The man used to be a Navy SEAL and escaped from a supermax prison. Not a lot these days can keep him under lock and key. Ben will know what to do with him."

"Is Ben bringing him here?"

"If Dupree ends up secured in Knoxville, I'm gonna meet Ben in St. Louis for the handoff."

"I'm going with you."

"St. Louis is a powder keg right now. Not safe, you're staying here."

"Max, don't make me say it."

"Elizabeth, I need you in charge here while I'm gone."

"I really need to say it?"

"Elizabeth, please."

"He killed our son, Maxwell! I'm coming with you!"

CHAPTER NINE

"You're insane."

"Dr. Biggs, while I will freely admit that I am a narcissistic sociopath, I am quite sane."

"Are you joking?"

"Far from it. The icepick lodged in Mr. McCallon's ear speaks to that point."

Sebastian had actually forgotten about the corpse still in the room. The fact that Charles knew his true identity was enough to make the good doctor forget every facet of reality. The entire reason Dr. Biggs abandoned his previous life was so that his extensive knowledge of artificial intelligence wouldn't fall into the wrong hands. The last thing the world needed was another up and coming dictator like the late Simon Sterling creating an artificially intelligent war machine. Sebastian never imagined his knowledge of aeronautics would attract anyone.

"Dr. Biggs, I can assume you have two very basic questions – how and why? Am I correct?"

"You could say that."

"Well, the reasons why I wish to embark on this endeavor need not concern you. How we will proceed from this point is quite the opposite."

"Do I have a choice?"

"Of course you do! Come now, Sebastian! I can't imagine you'd turn down such an opportunity."

"You'll forgive me if I doubt your abilities."

"I'd be concerned if you didn't. Trust me; your doubts will soon vanish."

"You say your reasons don't concern me. They concern me a great deal."

"And why is that, Sebastian?"

"You really think I'm naïve enough to believe your motivations for getting into space are for science? For the good of mankind?"

"My goodness, Sebastian, why else would I want to embark upon such a grand endeavor? Is it so hard to believe that an old man at the end of his life would aspire to achieve something so remarkable?"

"I find it very hard to believe that all you want is to scratch an entry off your bucket list."

"I'm sorry, and what is a 'bucket list'? I'm not familiar with the term."

"Really? You know, uh, things to do before you die … kick the bucket?"

"Ah, you Americans are so clever. I assume you're worrying my plans center around some nefarious purpose?"

"That sums it up, yes."

"I wonder, what evil plot can you envision?"

"Uh, well, I don't really know."

"Neither can I, Sebastian, neither can I. While I am very adept at killing, I don't know what it is you think I want to accomplish up there that would jeopardize mankind. I'm simply offering you the chance to reclaim the glory of your previous profession, the very notion of which you no doubt abandoned a long time ago. How can you turn down such an opportunity? Even if I'm a delusional old fool, what do you have to lose?"

"My time."

"Dr. Biggs, I'll be more than compensating you for your time."

"Which will be what?"

Charles looked to the floor. "A position of power here in St. Louis has become available."

Sebastian looked to the floor and back at Charles. "I like the sound of that."

"I'm honestly surprised to hear you say that so quickly, Sebastian. I thought it would require a lot more effort on my part. You've been in hiding for so long; I figured such a bright spotlight would be hard for you step into."

"That much power? Are you kidding? Being in charge of the last great city in America? Why would I need to hide?"

"A valid point. Good for you, sir."

"What about Willie's lieutenants?"

"Easily dispatched. I simply preyed upon their lust

for power. Each thought I was murdering Mr. McCallon on their behalf so they could take his place."

"That's what you were doing while I was out in the hallway guarding the door?"

"Precisely."

"No way Frank was on board."

"He wasn't. An unfortunate accident befell Willie's partner." Charles felt it imprudent to disclose the intimate details of Frank and Willie's sexual relationship. His professional standards would not allow such indiscretion.

"You've been planning this for a long time."

"Indeed, I have. You were the last piece of the puzzle."

"What would have happened to your plan if you couldn't find me?"

"Oh, Sebastian! Anyone can be found. All that is required is time and patience."

Sebastian could feel himself getting drunk with power and he liked it. "You've definitely got my attention. What do you need from me?"

"For now, only your patience. Do you play chess?"

"When I can find a worthy opponent, which is rare."

"Such arrogance, doctor! A trait I find endearing when deserved. As you know, the pawns are expendable, a means of drawing out your opponent so you can strike."

"I'm one of pawns then?"

Charles laughed. "Oh dear, Sebastian! If anything, you are the king. Far too important to fight and get your hands dirty. All you need to do is sit back and wait for the game to be won. That is the point I was trying to make. Right now the pawns are entrenched in battle. You see, this game was won before it even started. I already know what every piece is going to do before they do it. You and I just have to be patient while the game is played."

"And how long will that be?"

"Not long. We just have to wait for some of the key pieces to realize they are playing and make their move."

"You're not making a lot of sense."

"Suffice it to say, Sebastian, it would take far too long to explain and I don't want to bore you with the details."

"I do have one question."

"Hopefully I can provide an answer."

"Am I going to be your puppet? Why don't you just take control of St. Louis yourself? You don't need me."

"Do pay attention, doctor. I've already answered that question. If you recall, I told you that I am not a fan of St. Louis and I meant it. After our business is concluded, you can burn St. Louis to the ground for all I care, makes no difference to me. I am simply offering you payment for services to be rendered."

"Fair enough."

Charles stood and retrieved a pair of gloves from his pocket and put them on. Sebastian looked at him with confusion. The gray haired gentleman dropped down to one knee and placed his palm on Willie's forehead. "I'd say it's been long enough."

Sebastian was definitely confused. "For what?"

"This." Charles grabbed the icepick with his free hand and slowly retracted it from Willie's ear. "After enough time has elapsed, gravity takes over and blood pools at the lowest point." Charles pointed at the hole in Willie's ear. "See? No blood. If you are too quick to retract after the lethal blow, blood will pour out and make quite the mess. Drive it into the skull down to the hilt and very little blood spills. Much tidier this way."

"I really didn't need to know that."

"Nonsense, doctor, a man of science such as yourself? I thought men like you had a thirst for knowledge."

Sebastian's apprehension returned. "I don't need to know everything."

"There you go again, doctor! You need to relax! Sure you don't want to spit on him? Offer still stands."

Sebastian faked a smile. "I'm good, thanks."

CHAPTER TEN

Richard Dupree was learning very little from his captors. He had spent the night in the makeshift prison cell alongside the now stinking remains of the bounty hunter who sang like a bird about Richard's war criminal status and the large reward on his head. He had yet to see the "judge" he had heard so much about. The last bit of information he could glean from anyone was that the judge would see him in the morning. Beyond that, he had no idea what was in store. Richard could see nothing outside of his cell save for a few bullet holes in the ceiling. He spent the first few hours trying to politely engage in conversation with the people he assumed were still in the building. He wanted to get in their heads to get an idea of what was in store and to learn their weaknesses. *Please, you have to let me go. I haven't done anything wrong. I don't know why I'm here.* The classics didn't elicit a response so during the next few hours he graduated to the angrier protests. *You got the wrong guy! This isn't right! You can't do this to me! Let me out right now!* Human psychology was simple – everyone has a limit to the amount of aggravation they will tolerate before they snap. Richard had yet to find that limit.

If Richard had acquired more intel on these people he would try more drastic means to draw them into opening the cell door. Trying to break down the door or screaming like a madman might lead to a broken arm or a busted kneecap for his trouble and he needed to be whole for whatever came next. For now, his plan was to stay quiet and observe.

Footsteps could be heard in front of the cell. Someone kicked on the door. "Listen up, General! Step to the back of the cell. When the door opens you'll be lookin' at the business end of a shotgun. Do something stupid and your foot gets blown off!"

Richard grinned. "Virgil? Is that you? Now it's just my foot? Appreciate that. We friends now?"

"Shut the fuck up and get your ass in back of the cell, General."

"You got it, amigo." Richard stepped to the back of the cell.

Richard could hear locks and clasps clicking and finally the door opened. "Damn, General, a rottin' corpse in there with ya' and I'm pretty sure that's you I'm still smelling."

"Let me go and you won't have to smell me."

"You're way too valuable to let go. Gonna make some serious coin for your nasty ass."

"You're selling me into slavery? That's not very civilized."

"Knock that shit off. You know what's going on."

"Not really, no idea what I'm doing here."

"Well, General Dupree, you can tell it to the judge, he's ready to see you."

***

The Honorable Timothy Willock loved his job. He had never been to law school or worked a single day in the legal profession prior to his appointment to the bench. The best he could figure he possessed two qualities that got him to his current station in life – he was over the age of fifty and had a college degree. Timothy believed this rare pedigree could not be found anywhere in a twenty mile radius, maybe a hundred.

Judge Willock never had an issue with self-esteem; he was a confident man that had always been well liked. However, the god-like respect everyone showered on him was intoxicating. He lived for it. Since re-election had never been mentioned to him and no one else showed interest, he assumed it was a lifetime appointment. That suited him just fine. If old age or illness confined him to his bed, he would hold court in his bedroom.

Today's docket was particularly interesting. An infamous war criminal had been captured in his jurisdiction. When he read the wanted poster the bounty hunter all but thrust in his face he could hardly contain his excitement. This idiot had a badly broken hand and had the audacity to make demands.

"Your honor, I'm here on authority of Denver to bring this fugitive to justice. I've been granted full authority by Maxwell Harris himself to place General Dupree in custody and transport him to Denver."

Judge Willock mocked surprise. "Virgil! You hear that?"

Virgil was seated next to him reading the wanted poster. He was happy to play along. "Yes, sir, your honor. This guy's big shit, we better listen."

"Damn right, Virgil. Maxwell Harris himself! Wow! What should we do, Virgil?"

"Not really sure, Judge. Hey, by the way, where is Denver?"

Judge Willock bellowed out in laughter. "Oh, best I can figure, a long fuckin' way from here!"

The bounty hunter panicked. "Now look here, Judge, we can work this out. You need me; I know everything we gotta do. I can handle this whole thing for you, split it right down the middle."

"Virgil, we need him?"

"No, sir, Judge. I think we got this covered."

"Sorry, Virgil says we don't need you." Judge Willock looked at Virgil and cocked his eyes towards the bounty hunter. "You need someone with a broke up hand?"

"Shit no."

"Well, we can't have him makin' trouble for us and we can't have people come lookin' for him neither. See to that."

"Yes sir."

Judge Willock barely heard the bounty hunter's sobs as Virgil took him away. He couldn't take his eyes off the wanted poster. A hundred pounds of silver would go a long way to build his militia.

***

"General Dupree, at last we meet."

"Where's my lawyer?"

Judge Willock was genuinely amused. "Virgil, you

were right. This guy is something else."

Richard was on his knees with two sets of handcuffs securing his hands behind his back. Virgil was standing over him with a baseball bat. "Yes sir, your honor."

The judge peered over his glasses with condescension. "This is not the old world, General. I am your lawyer. My word is law. I don't need pesky windbags in here wasting my time. Are we clear?"

"Not really."

The judge scowled. Virgil knew what to do when the judge didn't look happy. He grabbed Dupree's long greasy hair and jerked his head back. "Mind your manners."

The judge continued, "General Richard Dupree, you stand accused of a very lengthy list of crimes: espionage, treason, escape, grand theft, and multiple counts of murder. You have anything to say?"

"Sure I do. You got the wrong guy, I'm innocent."

"Of course you are. Need I remind you, sir, the murder of Father Elias has been added to the list?"

"I already told Virgil here I tried to save Father Elias. The dead body in my cell is the one killed the priest."

"General, you are the reason the priest is dead. You must know that. I went to high school with Nathan. He was the last good man in these parts and he'd still be alive if not for you. Run your smart ass mouth to the contrary and you'll be spitting teeth."

Richard knew the judge was right. He wished he'd have never set foot in the church. "You're right. I'm sorry about the priest."

"You should be. Let's cut to the chase. I find you guilty."

Richard had no illusions that he would be given anything resembling a fair trial. "What happens now?"

"I've contacted one of Denver's allies. They will be taking custody and transporting you to Denver."

"After you've been paid off."

"Quite handsomely. Thank you."

"Let me guess, Benjamin Black?"

"As a matter of fact, yes. Friend of yours?"

"Me and Ben go way back."

"Well, General, I'm glad I could arrange your reunion. You'll be leaving with Virgil here within the hour. Rot in hell. Goodbye." Judge Willock banged his gavel. Virgil grabbed Richard by the hair and pulled him to his feet.

"Let's go fuckhead. Gotta get you ready."

Richard was led down the hallway behind the judge's bench to the area in front of his cell. Virgil pushed him into a folding chair and picked up a pitcher of water. "Drink."

Richard eyed Virgil with caution. "What is it?"

"It's water, dumbass. Gotta keep you alive. Once we hit the road, you won't be getting a drop." Virgil grabbed his chin and forced his mouth open.

"Okay, okay. I'll drink, don't force it." Virgil held the pitcher above his lips and slowly poured water down his throat.

As he was pouring, Virgil said, "You see, General, we got the skinny on how to handle you. Your buddy Ben told us how slippery you can be. Seems like you're a damn good escape artist." Once the pitcher was empty, Virgil pulled a dirty bandana out of his pocket and gagged Richard. "You won't be doin' no talking. Damn shame really, you're a pretty funny guy. Can't have you playin' your fancy mind games. Good ole' Ben says that's how you pulled off your last escape."

Richard was quite proud of his last escape. Six months prior one of Max's teams ambushed him while he was picking over a Walgreens for supplies. While en route to Denver, Richard simply played the fools against each other. At first they just argued with each other. Pretty soon the arguments escalated to shoving matches followed by fistfights. On the third day, all five of the men were at each other throats and no one bothered to look after Richard. He simply took off running and by the time his captors settled down, Richard was nowhere to be found.

Virgil opened a footlocker and retrieved a musty burlap sack. "Sorry about the smell, General. This here's the bag I use when I hunt squirrels and rabbits." Virgil slipped the bag over Richard's head and patted him on the shoulder. "Won't be taking in the sights neither. Gonna be a boring trip for you. Reckon you can catch up on some sleep."

For the first time in recent memory, Richard was not optimistic about his immediate future. Even in the most desperate of circumstances, he could find some small weakness and exploit it to control his fate. Decency could be met with violence. Any kindness paid to his humanity could be twisted into an opportunity. Richard's humanity had been replaced with a winning lottery ticket that Judge Willock was intent on cashing.

Virgil reached behind Richard's head and took a set of leg irons hanging on the wall. He securely fastened them and laughed. "Let me fill you on a little secret, General. You better hope your friend Ben has a cuff key to let you out of this iron 'cuz I ain't bringing one."

Richard was escorted out to the street and lifted up by four men into the back of a pickup. The sound of horses made it clear how the pickup was making the trip.

Virgil said, "What're we waitin' on?"

"Robbie and Seth are getting the food," someone said.

"What about feed for the horses?" asked Virgil.

Richard made note of another voice. "Can't we just let 'em graze?"

"No, retard. I want tight security. We all stick close together. Can't venture out looking for pasture. Take your stupid ass and get some feed. Hurry up."

The next few minutes were filled with silence as they waited for the provisions to arrive. To his right, Richard heard two of the men whispering.

"How much you gettin' paid?"

"Why?"

"Don't make no sense. Why we gotta split the payday thirteen ways? Shit, we can do the job with half that. More money in our pockets."

Virgil screamed, "Dipshits! We ain't even left yet and you fuckers done forgot the most important rule!"

"Damn, Virgil! What?"

"When you within earshot of the prisoner, don't talk! The fuck you say?"

Richard didn't hear a reply and imagined the two men staring at their feet hoping Virgil would leave them alone. The two men didn't need to say anything more; Richard had gathered the most crucial piece of intel he was after – how many trigger fingers were along for the ride.

Richard took inventory of the situation. Handcuffs and leg irons with no key, robbed of his sight and the ability to speak, and the grand prize – thirteen highly motivated men to watch over him.

He might have little choice but to pay Max a visit.

CHAPTER ELEVEN

Maxwell Harris had never been one for traveling. Prior to the collapse of 2027 during his career in law enforcement, his vacations consisted of remaining on the couch playing video games and binge-watching television shows. The idea of spending his hard-earned vacation days on a beach or a theme park was his vision of hell. His wife, on the other hand, loved to travel and in her own way considered their trip to St. Louis a sort of vacation. He was glad that at least one of them was going to enjoy the trip because he certainly was not. His back, hips, and left leg were in such bad shape that any sensible doctor would strongly advise him not to travel. The traitor had eluded Max for far too long so if the trip left him paralyzed, then so be it.

Elizabeth had all but emptied their home of every pillow, blanket, sheet, and towel and placed them in the back of a Ford Bronco. Max did not like being pampered. "Honey, this is too much. I don't need all of this."

"What you need is to stay here and let me be the one to go. But we both know that isn't going to happen so the least you can do is shut up and let me make you comfortable."

"Yes ma'am."

"You bring your medicine?"

"Yep, all of which expired twelve years ago."

"You really should stay here. I promise I won't kill Dupree."

"I'm more worried about him killing you and everyone on our team."

"Your confidence in my abilities is touching. Thank you."

Max winked. "You're welcome."

Elizabeth finished the makeshift bed and stepped back. "Your first-class accommodations await. Care to try it out?"

"Not till we leave. Once I get comfortable in there good luck getting me out."

"Good point. You are very lazy."

Max rolled his eyes. "You're funny.

"I've got everything under control so you might as well get in."

"Fuel?"

"Enough for the round trip and a little to spare. Using seventy-five percent of our supply."

"Weapons and ammo?"

"Twelve rifles, twelve pistols, twelve shotguns. The M-60 is mounted along with all the ammo we have for it."

"Food and water?"

"Max."

"Just answer the question, Elizabeth."

Elizabeth indulged her husband's incessant need for checklists. She huffed and answered in a dull monotone. "Four cases of MREs and thirty gallons of water."

"Thank you, dear. Was that so hard?"

"Will you please get in the car?"

"Yes ma'am." Max kissed his wife and climbed in the passenger seat and rolled down the window.

"Are you kidding me? I made that comfy bed and you're gonna sit up here?"

"Don't worry; I'll get back there when I need it. Let's get the team up here for a briefing."

Elizabeth waved over the other ten members of the team. They all gathered around Max's window.

"Okay people, listen up. Some introductions are in order. We are lucky to have Isaac Lynwood and three of his people with us. Isaac was responsible for bringing Theo back to us. One of the last things Theo told me was to trust Isaac and that we could count on him. I don't know about any of you, but if Theo vouched for him, he's one of us."

"Thank you, Max, I appreciate that. Whatever you need, brother. We're ready."

Max continued, "This will be just like a recon mission or supply run but a hell of a lot longer. Four vehicles with teams of three in each. Open road with high visibility you spread out, tighter roads with low visibility you get closer. A lot of desperate people out there will do anything to get their hands on this much fuel so watch out for Good Samaritan traps. That means no stopping for anyone. You will radio in your fuel status on every quarter mark. The only bathroom break you're getting is when we stop to refuel so you better bring a piss jug. Since we don't travel further than fifty miles out, we'll be setting up camp before the sun goes down. We will not be driving in the dark. Since Isaac and his people are joining us, let's go over the rules of engagement. Someone on foot starts firing, just keep on driving and return fire only it's needed to get away, otherwise, save your ammo. If we're attacked by another vehicle or group of vehicles, you are clear to engage but be mindful of friendly fire and do not stop unless you have no other choice. I'll be in the lead so if we come up on any roadblocks, it will be my call. If a vehicle is disabled, we all stop and form a perimeter around it. Questions?"

Several members of the team looked at each other waiting for someone to ask the question on all of their minds. Finally, someone spoke up. "What's in St. Louis, boss? Why are we going?"

"I won't be answering that until we stop to refuel. Until then, don't dwell on it and stay focused. Any more questions? If not, we're burning daylight."

Max caught a break and had heard from Benjamin Black early that morning confirming that he had Dupree in custody and was en route to St. Louis. Max was not expecting to hear from Ben until noon and had planned on leaving at sunrise the next day. With plenty of daylight in front of them, they left shortly after breakfast. Close to nine hundred miles of hostile road stood between Max and Richard. Prior to the collapse, the trip could be made in roughly fourteen hours. Eleven years of decay meant long stretches of barely passable roads. Four years of war with the Chinese meant bombed out cities and bridges long since destroyed. Desperation meant packs of violent thugs happy to relieve you of your possessions and leave you for dead. Max would be happy to make two hundred miles a day which meant four days to St Louis. Max had told Ben that if he didn't make contact by sunrise in seven days to execute Dupree. Max needed the assurance that if he couldn't make it to St. Louis alive that Dupree would get what he had coming to him.

The first day of the journey was surprisingly uneventful. After they left the compound, they didn't see another human being the entire day. The main issue they had to contend with was maintaining a steady speed on the road. Abandoned cars littered the road so it just wasn't safe to drive fifty miles an hour since you never knew what was over the next hill or around the bend. They also had to contend with potholes that could chew a tire to shreds. Thirty miles an hour was about as fast as Max was willing to risk when the road allowed, which wasn't often. In three different sections the road was completely blocked with abandoned cars so they had to cross the median to the westbound lanes to get around it. Twice they came upon collapsed bridges and had to backtrack to find suitable terrain that would allow them to navigate around and get back to the road. The most difficult task of the day was spent dealing with a cell phone tower that had fallen across all four lanes of traffic. They made just shy of two hundred miles before nightfall and made camp.

The second day proved to be more eventful. Two hundred seventy five miles east of Denver on Interstate 70, the eastbound lanes were backed up as far as the eye could see. To make matters worse, the westbound lanes were also backed up with vehicles heading east. Isaac was driving the lead vehicle and Max was next to him in the passenger seat.

"Son of a bitch," said Max.

"What do you wanna do, boss?" said Isaac.

"Elizabeth," said Max as he looked up.

"Got it." Elizabeth exited the vehicle and climbed up on the roof with a pair of binoculars. "It's bad, I can't see past it. A lot of old school buses back here near us but it's mainly a military convoy."

"Ours?"

"Not PSA, it's Chinese."

"Chinese? Heading east?" asked Isaac.

"Look like some epic battle happened here?" asked Max.

"Hard to say from back here. We could ask General Dupree, brilliant military leader and all."

"I'm sure he'll tell us all about it," said Max. "Can we get around it?"

"Not looking that way."

Max keyed up his radio. "Everyone rally on me."

Less than a minute later the other nine members of the team were gathered around Max's window. "Hanson, take your team up a few hundred yards and scout the area. We need a way around this disaster. Got your binoculars?"

Hanson nodded.

"Good, if you come up empty then double time it back here for plan B."

Elizabeth asked, "What's plan B?"

"I'm sure we'll think of something before they get back."

"Oh honey, Leadership 101, come on. Lie and say you have a plan."

Max deadpanned. "I have a plan."

Isaac bellowed out in laughter, which relaxed everyone enough to let out a few chuckles. Max smiled and winked to the rest of the team. "Seriously, I have a basic idea that's going to depend on what intel they find. Everyone relax, I know what I'm doing."

"We know you do, brother, we know you do," said Isaac.

Max said, "Mr. Hanson, stay in contact on the radio and tell us what you see. We need some good news."

"I'll do my best, boss."

Hanson and his team returned to their vehicle and retrieved their gear. They made it past the lead vehicle and disappeared into the vehicle graveyard blocking their way. About five minutes later, Max heard the radio transmit. "Hanson to Max."

"Go."

"No signs of a firefight. No bullet holes, no shell casings. Haven't seen a single corpse so far. Just empty vehicles."

"Tell me what vehicles you see."

"As you guys can see from back there, school buses, city buses. Then we've got five-ton trucks, tanks, APCs, Humvees, and some more shit. Got a hill a few minutes in front of us. Once we get to the top, we should know what we're dealing with."

"Copy that, we'll be standing by."

Isaac asked, "How's that plan of yours looking?"

"We'll know at the top of the hill."

A few minutes passed and Hanson called in his report. "You're not gonna believe this shit. A train derailed on to the fucking highway. A giant ass crater is sitting where the train tracks should be and the train just spilled out on to the road. Can't see past the train wreckage but that doesn't really matter."

"Why?" asked Max.

"A serious battle took place here. Looks like the Chinese were trying to salvage what was on the train and the PSA bombed the shit out of them. Either side of the highway is nothing but bomb craters, dead bodies, and wrecked vehicles. You want my opinion?"

"Of course I do."

"Chinese tried to retreat and didn't make it. Total slaughter."

"Sounds like it. You see a way for us to get around?"

"Certainly not looking good from where I'm standing."

"How far up is the train wreck?"

"At least a mile."

"Okay then, head on back."

"Copy that."

Elizabeth was standing at the driver's side window with Isaac. She looked at her husband. "Max, what's the plan?"

"We can't get around this mess, so we have to find a way through it."

Elizabeth was confused. "And just how do we do that?"

"You're not gonna like it."

"What?"

"First, I have to turn around and head back to Denver. No way in hell I'm making it over a mile in my condition. The rest of you head up on foot and acquire new transportation."

"You're staying with us," said Elizabeth.

"You need to be reasonable. You know that's not going to happen."

"Can we carry him?" asked Isaac.

Max was losing patience. "No! You can't carry me. I have a fucked up spine and I'll end up in worse shape before we get there. It was stupid of me to come in the first place."

"Honey, are you done?" Elizabeth was smiling at her husband. She held her smile and waited for him to calm down.

Max sighed and rolled his eyes. "You brought it didn't you? I told you not to bring it and you brought it anyway."

"Brought what?" asked Isaac.

"His wheelchair," said Elizabeth.

The other members of the team exchanged puzzled looks. None of them had seen Max in a wheelchair and they looked to each other for confirmation. *Wheelchair? Have you ever seen him in a wheelchair?* Max looked around and could tell what was going on.

"No," said Max.

"You're really going to let your stubborn pride keep you from Dupree?" asked Elizabeth.

Max remained silent.

"That's what I thought." Elizabeth walked to the third SUV and opened the rear hatch. She moved some boxes around and found the wheelchair still hidden under a blanket right where she left it. She unfolded it and pushed it to the front of the convoy. Max opened his door and stood next to the wheelchair. He glared at it like he was in the death chamber about to be strapped into the electric chair. He finally sat down and became very sullen, not because he had admitted defeat and surrendered to the wheelchair, it was because he was contemplating his words.

"I was the vice president of the Pacific States of America right up to the day she fell and I was never told about this. If I didn't know anything about it that means Marshall Beck didn't either."

The members of the team, Elizabeth included, rarely heard Max speak the name of Howard Beck's son, who was also the second president of the PSA.

No one moved a muscle, they hung on Max's every word. "I want to know what happened here. I want to know what was on that train and I want to know why Richard never told us about it."

CHAPTER TWELVE

"I gotta tell ya, Richard, you've seen better days. Known you a lot of years and I never seen you with a beard and your hair ain't never been more than an inch long. Nice look you got going."

"Thank you, Ben. You wanna braid it? Talk about boys?"

"Fuck you, Richard."

Richard smiled at the playful banter. He paused for a minute and said, "I'm glad it was you."

"What?"

"I'm glad you were the one that caught me."

"Why is that?"

"I'm still alive."

"I have a feeling that will change, Richard."

"I'm sure it will. Max would've killed me by now."

"Why is that? You two were like brothers."

"Is the face guard and straight jacket really necessary, Ben? I mean, sure, I get that I'm a dangerous lunatic and all, but the whole *Silence of the Lambs* thing is a bit much."

"You make Hannibal Lecter look like a simpleton, so cut the shit, it's not coming off."

"Loved the book, you read it?"

"Stop it, Richard. Don't change the subject. What the hell happened with you two?"

"Long story."

"St. Louis is at least another hour away. Plenty of time to take a trip down memory lane."

"When Max sees me, I'm sure you'll figure it out."

"Richard, my old friend, I have a front row seat and I wouldn't miss it for the world."

Richard wasn't sure how many vehicles were in Ben's convoy. The blindfold came off and all he could see one SUV in front. The face guard was fastened to the straightjacket so he couldn't turn his head. Ben had a goon armed with a taser sitting on either side of Richard while Ben road shotgun. Richard was very impressed; Ben came prepared.

"Ben, can I ask you a question?"

"You can ask, don't mean I'll answer."

"How is Max? Is he okay?"

"Like you give a shit."

"Ben, please. Just because he wants me dead doesn't mean I feel the same. How is he?"

"Have you ever known him to be in good health? I haven't."

"He's had his ups and down."

"Well, it's been nothing but down since you left. The drinking's been really bad. I know it's about the best thing to escape this shitty world and we all do it more than we should, but Max gives new meaning to the term 'functioning alcoholic.' You ask me, it's a really slow way to commit suicide. To make things even worse, he can barely walk."

"What? He got than fancy surgery from Hal…"

"Don't say his name! Say his name one more fucking time and…"

"Okay, sorry. I won't."

"Yes, he had the surgery but it wasn't enough. Permanent nerve damage, he's in constant pain. Only gets worse when he's active. Thanks to your stupid ass, medical intervention isn't really an option."

Richard had had enough. Ben spoke the hurtful truth and Richard didn't want to hear another word of it. Ben looked at him in the rear view mirror and saw the look of defeat in Richard's eyes. Satisfied with his victory, Ben changed the subject.

"What the hell have you been doing all this time? I mean, other than running?"

"You wouldn't believe me if I told you."

"Try me."

"Wait, you need to know something."

"Huh?"

"Whatever's about to happen, I had nothing to do with it."

Ben swung around in his seat and looked directly

at Richard. "The fuck you talking about?" Before Ben could turn around and face forward, the lead vehicle veered off the road and flipped over in the ditch. Ben grabbed the rifle between his legs. "Drive! Drive! Drive!"

The driver slammed the accelerator to the floor and the SUV lurched forward.

Richard was eerily calm. "I'd pull over if I were you."

Ben didn't take his eyes off the road. "Dammit, Dupree! What the hell did…"

The driver's head erupted and covered Ben's face in brain matter. The bullet then exited the driver's head and came to a stop in the throat of the man sitting next to Richard.

Richard screamed, "Ben! Take the wheel!"

Ben wiped the blood from his eyes and grabbed the wheel, desperately trying to keep the SUV on the pavement. Thankfully, the driver had slumped forward and his foot slid off the accelerator. When the vehicle had slowed enough, Ben carefully steered it down a gentle slope and into some bushes. The front bumper nudged into a tree and they stopped.

Richard's tactical assessment completely changed in less than thirty seconds. He had previously hoped that Ben's convoy was small and only one vehicle was behind them. When Ben opened the rear door and pulled him out, Richard wanted nothing more than to see an army of vehicles engaging whatever force had attacked them.

The road was empty. They were alone.

Ben flung Richard to the ground and stepped on his neck. The man that was sitting to Richard's right foolishly ran from cover and was gunned down. "God damn you, Richard! No way your buddies are getting you out of here! I'll kill you first!"

"This ain't me. Why would I warn you ahead of time?"

A canister hit the roof of the SUV and bounced a few feet away from Ben and Richard. A deafening boom and a shower of sparks disoriented Ben. He dropped his rifle and instinctively brought his hands to his ears. Before he could react, Ben was punched in the face and brought to the ground by three men. Bound by a straightjacket, all Richard could do was watch. He looked up to see an old man walking towards him. Once he was close enough, Richard could see that the man was smiling.

"Hello there! I apologize for all the theatrics, not really my style. Such a racket! Bullets whizzing everywhere, car crashes, far too much excitement for this old man." The old man took off his sunglasses and knelt down. "Oh my! Look at you! Are you on your way to a sanatorium?"

Richard stared up at the man in bewilderment.

"The looney bin? I must admit I can't recall the last time I saw a straightjacket. Looks to be quite effective."

Richard was still speechless.

"Where are my manners? Goodness! My name is Charles. I trust you are Richard Dupree?"

Richard managed to nod his head.

"Are you injured, sir? Can you speak?" Charles smiled and showed genuine concern, which troubled Richard.

"I think I'm okay."

"Good! Let's get some of the formalities out of the way. Is it 'Mr. Dupree,' or 'General Dupree?'"

"I really don't care."

"Call that motherfucker 'General.' He needs to own the horrible shit he did," said Ben.

"Let's not be crude, sir. And who might you be?"

"Fuck you."

Charles frowned and nodded. One of the men restraining Ben drove his fist down on Ben's mouth. Charles held up his hand. "Your name, sir."

"Benjamin Black!"

The smile quickly returned to Charles' face. "Are you *the* Benjamin Black? The one that ran that fabulous little compound at Disney World?"

Ben glared at Charles and rolled his eyes.

"A real pleasure, sir. I never thought I'd actually get the chance to meet you! What a small world! Isn't this fun?"

"Do I know you?" asked Ben.

"No, I'm afraid not. I am very familiar with you, however. I was kind enough to deliver Jackson Butler to you on a silver platter."

"Is that a fact?"

"It is indeed."

"Is that supposed to make us friends?"

"I wish it did, Mr. Black, I really do. Such a shame we had to meet this way. The world needs men like you, now more than ever." Charles stood and calmly produced the same icepick that had scrambled Willie McCallon's brains.

"Stop!" screamed Richard.

Ben said, "Cut the shit, Richard, it's pathetic. I knew I was dead the second your friends attacked us."

"Ben, I swear to you I had nothing to do with this! They're not my friends!"

"He's right, Mr. Black. General Dupree had no prior knowledge of this encounter." Charles held up the icepick signaling for his men to hold Ben down. "General, please observe, I want you to witness this. I was having a friendly chat a dear friend you will soon meet. You only need watch."

Charles thrust the icepick into Ben's ear and quickly pulled it out. Ben twitched for a few seconds and then his eyes rolled back in his head. A few drops of blood slowly trickled out of his ear and ran down his cheek.

"Oh dear, this is rather embarrassing. For some reason I remember this being much messier. I told the good doctor that blood would spurt out of the ear. On second thought, General, I'd appreciate if you didn't mention this to Dr. Biggs. I'm afraid I'd just look downright silly."

Richard closed his eyes, a single tear streaked down his cheek. Once again, a good man had died because of him.

"General, you surprise me! I just liberated you from your captor. I thought you'd be grateful."

"He was a good man! He didn't deserve to die like that! The least you could have done was let the man keep an ounce of dignity, you're a monster!"

"Dignity is never found in death, General Dupree. The end result is always the same no matter how it is done. Proud and resolute or crying and whimpering, death doesn't discriminate."

"Just before I kill you, I think you'll change your mind."

Charles put his sunglasses back on and smiled. "General, I'm seventy-four years old. I've escaped death more times than I can remember but I do know that each time dignity was the furthest thing from my mind. Dignity is for the benefit of the murderer, not the victim."

"We'll see."

"General, let's put all this nastiness behind us think of more pleasant things. We have a grand reception planned for you in St. Louis. You will be my honored guest. I pride myself on being a hospitable host. We'll get you cleaned up, nice shave and a haircut, you'll be a new man!"

Richard glared at Charles with intense hatred and talked through gritted teeth. "I like my hair, thank you very much."

"Whatever suits you, General. I must insist, however, that at the very least we wash it. We have some fabulous girls that can elevate your current level of hygiene to acceptable standards."

"You mean slaves?"

"By definition, yes, but I don't think they object to their station in life. They are treated quite well."

"People tend to take care of their property, of course they're treated well. Mind telling me what this is all about?"

"In due time, General, in due time. Just know that you and your friends are going to help me save the world."

"I don't have any friends."

"Of course you do, General, I've already arranged a pleasant little dinner party. While you are getting cleaned up, I'll be collecting the final guest. I just love reuniting old friends!"

CHAPTER THIRTEEN

Maxwell Harris was in a losing battle with his ego. For many years he had told himself that submitting to a wheelchair meant the end of his miserable life was near. Sheer defiance was the only thing that kept him out of the chair. The decaying world around him was not handicap accessible. He couldn't enjoy the convenience of a blue placard hanging from the rear-view mirror. A wheelchair meant he had to depend on others and Max had a difficult time making such a concession. Being a leader and delegating tasks was one thing, but relying on others to care for you like a parent cares for an infant was a concept Max was not willing to adopt. The wheelchair would be discarded as soon as it was practical to do so.

Max was currently seated in the wheelchair Elizabeth had managed to smuggle along for the trip. Three of his men were currently carrying Max over a ten yard stretch of inhospitable terrain. Max tried to dismiss the thought that his group would already be at the train wreckage if he wasn't slowing them down.

"Okay, put me down," said Max. The three men carefully set the wheelchair on the ground and Elizabeth instinctively took her place behind Max and pushed him forward.

Elizabeth leaned forward and whispered, "Sweetie, you need to stop pouting."

"I'm not pouting."

"Yes, you are. You're acting like a child."

"I feel like a child in this thing."

"Stop it! You need to accept the fact that you can't get around on your own. You of all people should know that in this terrible world we live in you have to be willing to adapt to survive. Why are you so against a wheelchair? What's really going on?"

"It makes me look weak and vulnerable. What good am I if I can't stand on my own two feet?"

"Hate to break it to you, sweetie, you've never been a kick ass and take names kind of guy. What makes you strong is what's in here." Elizabeth playfully slapped her husband's head.

"Ouch! Knock it off!"

"Shut up or I'll push you over a cliff."

Max smiled at the thought of how much he loved his wife. She had a way of putting things in perspective and didn't hesitate to call him out when he was being stubborn and stupid. He'd be lost without her. They continued on for another thirty minutes. Along the way, they had to stop two more times and carry Max as they did before. Each time, Max felt humiliated and angry for being a burden. He tempered the strain on his ego by reflecting on what his wife had said to him. His strength resided in his ability to be an intelligent leader. As much as he hated to admit it, he could accomplish the task from a wheelchair.

They stopped about a hundred feet from the derailed train. Everyone was silently waiting for instructions from Max. Everyone thought Max was quietly contemplating the wreckage in front of them. Elizabeth knew better, her husband was in horrible pain. She could see the vacant stare in his eyes. The only reality he was experiencing was agony. Max was alone in his own world. She and every member of their party had been stripped away. The sun beating down on his face did not register in his senses. The tons of twisted steel in front of him had vanished. Pain was the only thing that existed for him, nothing else. She had seen this many times and from horrible experience knew the only thing to do was wait. He would fight his way back and rejoin them.

Isaac was the first to speak. "Boss, I count eighteen cars that survived the crash. The front car looks to be demolished on the other side of the crater, not much we can do about that. What are your orders?"

Elizabeth looked at Max, hoping he would reply. His eyes were still vacant. She put her hand on his shoulder and squeezed. "Honey?"

Max flinched and blinked his eyes. "What?"

"Sweetheart, Isaac is talking to you."

Max closed his eyes and cleared his throat.

"What was that, Isaac?"

Isaac gave Elizabeth a concerned look. "Eighteen cars intact. What do you want us to do?"

"Elizabeth will stay here with me. Isaac, pick one person and scout ahead for reliable transportation so we can get the hell out of here. The rest of you, divide up in teams of two and start searching. Anything that gives us an idea what happened here I want to know it. Take any supplies you find useful. If you find any large stockpiles, let me know and we'll figure out a way to get what we can out of here when we leave. Let's go, get to work."

Everyone set about their task and Elizabeth waited for them to get out of earshot so she could speak privately with Max. "How bad is it?"

"I told you not to bring this damned thing."

"What's done is done. How bad is it?"

"My back feels like it's been hit repeatedly with a sledgehammer and the bones in my legs feel like they're on fire. You know, a typical day."

"Got any candy on you?"

Max reached in his vest pocket and pulled out a bottle. "Never leave home without it."

"You take any today?"

"Well, I was waiting 'till it got bad enough. Now seems as good a time as any." Max took two pills out of the bottle, popped them in his mouth, and gulped them down with the whiskey in his flask.

"Sweetie, you really think those expired meds do any good?"

"It loses some of its kick, but it still works. Even if it's just a placebo effect, I'll take it." Max gulped down the rest of the whiskey. "No placebo effect here, that's for damned sure."

Elizabeth frowned. "Good."

"What?"

"You finished your booze."

Max thought of the bottle of vodka in his pack and decided to keep his mouth shut. It was the same argument they'd had for years. Max sincerely believed that alcohol was the best painkiller he had at his disposal and getting drunk was just a beneficial side effect. Elizabeth, on the other hand, didn't subscribe to this theory and branded her husband a full-blown alcoholic who made the conscious choice to stay drunk as much as possible.

"What's your plan if Isaac can't find us a ride?"

Max was glad the subject had changed. "The only thing we can do, turn around and go back to our vehicles and find another way to St. Louis."

"I don't think you're up to that."

"Whether or not I'm up to it doesn't matter. Why don't you do a quick search out here for supplies. Lot's of military vehicles, bound to be weapons and ammo. Maybe some MREs if we're lucky."

"Good idea, I'm on it." Elizabeth took off her backpack and emptied the contents in a pile next to Max. "If we're lucky, I can fill this baby up with some goodies."

Elizabeth set about her task and went vehicle to vehicle searching for anything useful. She managed to find a few pistols, a tool kit, and two cases of MREs that could feed their team for an extra couple of days. While she was searching, Max managed to drink a quarter of the bottle of vodka. When the vodka managed to induce a wave of relaxation, Max put the bottle away just in time before he saw Elizabeth running towards him. She was smiling and very excited.

"Baby, you're not gonna believe what I found!"

"What?"

"A truck filled with medical supplies! I was digging around and hit the jackpot! I found a footlocker filled with those little morphine packs they give to combat medics! I can't believe it!"

Elizabeth emptied out her backpack next to Max and did the same with his. Max had wrapped the bottle of vodka in a shirt so thankfully Elizabeth didn't see it. He had never felt so happy in his entire life. Max had accepted the fact that he would never be able to manage the chronic pain that tormented him every second of every day. He could stop drinking and regain the sobriety that had been missing for years.

Elizabeth returned a few minutes later with two very full backpacks and dumped them in a pile close to Max. "I took the vials out of the packaging and got all of it. When we get a chance, we can inventory it and come up with a schedule and ration it out so it will last as long as possible."

"Thinking the same thing. Good idea."

"Want some now?"

"No, the pills I took are kicking in. I'll take some when I need it."

"Anybody checked in yet? They find anything?"

"No, haven't seen anybody moving around for quite a while."

"Want me to go check on them?"

"Let's give them a little while longer."

"Okay, still got some searching to do in that medical truck. Might find some more treasure."

"Yeah, no telling what's in there."

Elizabeth had been gone a few minutes when Max heard footsteps to his right. The sun was directly in his eyes so he couldn't make out who was coming toward him. "Hanson? Is that you?"

"No, Mr. Harris, I'm afraid Mr. Hanson and the rest of your team will not be joining us."

Upon hearing an unfamiliar voice making such a claim, Max instinctively grabbed his pistol. Before he could raise his sidearm, a bullet tore through the armrest of his wheelchair. A split second later, another bullet kicked up dirt directly in front of him. Max let go of his pistol and slowly raised his hands. He did not dare move another inch.

"Mr. Harris, I have every intention of keeping you alive. My two associates are quite talented at long range shooting. Should you feel the need to touch that nasty little gun of yours, you can rest assured you will lose a hand. Are we clear?"

After a few steps, the figure speaking to him finally came into focus. A gray-haired man in an expensive suit was standing in front of him. He had a welcoming smile on his face, but his cold, dead eyes made Max uneasy. "Who are you? What's this all about? Where are my people?"

"So many questions, Mr. Harris! I suppose good manners should come first. My name is Charles, a real pleasure to meet you. As to my purpose, that will be made clear to you when the time is right. Your people? Well, I am sorry to say I had to kill them. Just don't have the resources to entertain so many guests. Quite pleased that I was able to kill them all by myself. I like to exercise my abilities when I can. At my age, it's a skill set that easily fades if not properly used from time to time."

Max slowly titled his head. "Elizabeth! If you can hear me, run! Get out of here as fast you can! Save yourself!"

"Mr. Harris, maybe I wasn't clear the first time. All of your people are dead. You are the only person I am interested in."

"Bullshit! You're lying!"

"I frown on vulgarity, sir. Let's keep a civil tongue."

"Whatever you say, you old geezer. She wasn't in the train. I know you're lying."

"How long have you been in the wheelchair? I'm aware of your medical concerns but the wheelchair surprises me. Are you okay?"

"Are you kidding? You murder my people and you expect chit chat! What is wrong with you?"

"I understand how you'd be upset, Mr. Harris. If you could just humor me and answer the question. I need to know if we need to make accommodations for you when we get to St. Louis."

Max tried his best to put on a poker face. *Did he know we were going to St. Louis or is it just a strange coincidence?* "I can get around, don't do me any favors."

"Fair enough. I am curious about something. How on earth did you plan to get it off the train and take it out of here? It doesn't appear that you came prepared. Not that it really matters, I retrieved it weeks ago."

"What are you talking about? Get what out of

here?"

"Don't be silly, Mr. Harris. We both know why you came here. What harm is it to tell me your plan now that it has obviously failed? I clearly beat you to it."

"I have no idea what you're talking about."

Charles walked up to Max and knelt down in front of his wheelchair. For Max, it was degrading, like a grownup kneeling down to be eye level with a child. He stared directly at Max for five very long and uncomfortable seconds. "Come now, Mr. Harris. Let's not play this game, it's a waste of time and insults us both."

"I had no idea any of this was even here until we stumbled upon it."

"You expect me to believe that? You came all this way from Denver and just found it by accident? Mr. Harris, I knew you were coming here to take it. I set a trap for you and waited."

"Listen to me, you old fart, I don't know how many times you want me to say the same thing. I have no idea what you're talking about!"

Charles studied Max intently for a few more seconds and started to laugh. "You really don't know, do you?"

Max said nothing.

"Oh my! I'm at a loss for words. All these years I thought you wanted Dupree's head because of what happened here. Dupree really didn't tell you, did he?"

Max glared at Charles with intense hatred. He did not like being made a fool, especially by this geriatric psycho. "Tell me what?"

"My good man, the end of the world started right here!"

Part 2 - 2034
The Final Days of the Chinese War

CHAPTER FOURTEEN

"Mr. President, sir, General Dupree's jet has landed, would you like for the General to report directly to you or does he have time to settle in his quarters?"

"Thank you, Hal. Please inform the General to report to me in fifteen minutes."

President Marshall Beck sat in the command center of Beck Castle, the stronghold built by his father decades ago to survive the end of the world, which it did for the most part in 2027. Anarchy and chaos had fractured the former United States and the deal was sealed when the Great Empire of Iran set off an electromagnetic pulse in the atmosphere above the eastern coast. From the ashes rose two opposing sides: the Pacific States of America, founded by his father, and the Unified American Empire, the result of a coup de tat orchestrated by Simon Sterling after he assassinated the last legitimate president, Malcolm Powers. The PSA managed to defeat the UAE only to face a bigger foe, the Chinese. The PSA had been battling the Chinese on their own soil for six long and bloody years.

"Hal, I'm finished with my coffee, I'm ready for the morning briefing."

"Yes, sir. General Dupree has requested to give you the briefing in person. Is that acceptable or would you still like to hear it?"

"That's fine, I can wait on Richard."

"In the meantime, sir, would you like to review your speech?"

"No, I don't."

"Are you sure, sir?"

"Hal, I've memorized every word of it. I'm good."

"Very well, sir."

"How are you doing on this fine morning my friend?"

"Sir, I am operating at peak capacity, performing seven hundred septillion operations per second. I am what you would consider 'present' at over sixty-two thousand locations simultaneously. I am currently piloting over three thousand craft and operating over eleven thousands robots. My diagnostic report—"

"Okay, Hal, that sounds great. Glad to know you're in tip-top shape."

"Thank you, sir."

"Please invite the vice-president to the meeting."

"That will not be necessary, sir. Vice President Harris is currently with General Dupree. The general has already extended an invitation."

"Perfect. I can't wait."

***

Richard Dupree opened the door to his quarters to find the grumpy scowl of his best friend.

"Max! How are you?" The two men embraced. Richard was smiling, Max was not.

"Take it easy, brother," grunted Max.

Richard took a step back. "Not doing so well, huh?"

"Typical day, no worse for wear."

Max took a step inside and Richard closed the door. "I'm changing into my fatigues and heading to meet the boss. You coming?"

"Sure, care to give me a sneak peek on your briefing?"

"Not a chance, Mr. Vice President."

"Fine, be that way."

Richard laced up his boots and headed to the door. Both men headed down the corridor and got on the elevator. Once at the command level, they made their way down another busy corridor to the outer chamber of the command center. Hal was kind enough to allow people to come and go throughout the stronghold based on their security clearance, however, the one door Hal would never open automatically was the one they were currently standing in front of.

While they were waiting, Max leaned over and whispered, "Come on, at least tell me if he's going to be happy."

"Marshall may share a few traits with his father, but he has one thing the old man never had."

"What?"

"Brilliant as he was, Howard had the emotional maturity of a teen-aged girl. Marshall can take bad news in stride."

"So it is bad news, then?"

"Shut up, wait and see."

"I outrank you, you know. Show a little respect."

"Okay, shut up, Mr. Vice President."

"That's better."

After a couple of hisses and a warning siren, the door to the command center creaked open. The massive doors retracted just enough to allow the two men to enter. Once they stepped in, the doors sealed shut.

Marshall Beck had been the youngest man to hold the office of president. Upon his father's death, Marshall took the oath of office and declared that the Pacific States of America to be the direct descendant of the United States of America. Based upon that proclamation, Howard Beck was the forty-seventh president and he was the forty-eighth. Marshall was thirty-nine years old when he took office. Six years in office had aged him at least twenty years.

Marshall extended his hand. "Richard, good to have you home."

"Mr. President, it's good to be home. Four weeks on the front lines was tough." Richard shook the president's hand with his right and clasped the president's forearm with his left.

"Hope you don't think this is a vacation, General. We've got work to do."

"Oh, I was thinking about taking a cruise. You know, since the last one went so well." Richard winked at Max. The last time the two men were on a cruise ship together, a Chinese submarine sank it.

Marshall rolled his eyes and smirked. "Sit down, both of you."

The president sat in his chair while the other two men retrieved chairs from the opposite wall. Once all three of them were in front of the spherical monitor, Marshall turned to Richard. "What do you have for me, General?"

Richard didn't waste time. "Hal, load my mission briefing and skip to part two."

"Of course, sir." A map of the North American continent spilled out in front of them on the holographic monitor. The Rocky Mountains served as the border between both sides. General Dupree had managed to bridge the gap between Washington state and Alaska, controlling the western edge of Canada. The Canadian government had crumbled more than a decade prior so the feat was an easy one. The PSA also controlled the entirety of the Baja peninsula solely for its strategic value in securing the Pacific Ocean, the rest of Mexico being a wasteland.

The three men studied the map while Richard spoke. "Mr. President, Mr. Vice-President, I present to you Operation Miraflores." Upon Richard's verbal cue, the map panned to the Panama Canal and zoomed in. "As we all know, the Chinese base their entire American Theater around the Panama Canal. With the Empire of Iran controlling the Middle East, Africa, and most of Europe, the Chinese are forced across the Pacific where they have to funnel over eighty percent of their manpower and resources through the canal. Once they are safely in the Caribbean, they either make their way into the Gulf of Mexico and up the Mississippi or they go around Florida and make their way up the coast."

The president held up his hand. "Richard, I want that canal intact."

"As do I, Mr. President. It's far too important. Even if we destroyed it, we'd still be fighting a desperate, wounded animal for eighteen months. I wouldn't be surprised if they nuked us all to hell on their way out the door. If we manage to beat them, we still have Iran to contend with and we need Panama to stay like it is."

Max punched Richard's arm.

"What the hell?" said Richard.

"'If we manage to beat them?'"

Richard sat back in his chair and paused in silent reflection. He looked at both men with an intensity that made them both uncomfortable. "That's what I said. Look, if the two of you want to fire me, then so be it. Make no mistake, gentlemen; we are losing this war, badly. Anything we send over the Rocky Mountains does not return and we can't move our navy across Mexico to get to the Gulf. All we have done for the past year is lick our wounds while they dig in deeper and wait for more men and resources to arrive. If we stay the course, we will lose, that is a fact."

The president held up his hand again. "Fair enough, General. Tell us your plan."

"It's right there on the screen, do you see it?"

Max waited for the president to speak. When Marshall looked to Richard impatiently, Max decided to intervene. "I see a heavily fortified canal and a blockade stretching from Columbia to Costa Rica."

Richard smiled. "You're looking on the wrong side."

The president sighed. "Really, Richard? The Caribbean? That's insane. We've been over this before. We don't have a single boat in the water and the Chinese are dug in deep. We know they'll never surrender it to us, they'll destroy the locks on the Pacific side and put the south end of the canal underwater. It would take decades to restore it."

"That's just the thing, gentlemen, we've been looking at this whole thing the wrong way. We don't need boats to capture the Panama Canal."

Marshall Beck was getting visibly upset. "I might take you up on your offer to get fired, this better be good."

"It is, Mr. President, but it's not without risk. We already know from previous failed missions that Hal's robots and his craft emit a carrier signal while not in stealth mode. We also know that when he's in stealth mode, the only thing he is capable of is reconnaissance. If he wants to engage the enemy he has to decloak. When that happens, the Chinese are immediately aware of our presence and the mission is short lived. The Chinese also have the airspace above the blockade monitored up to thirty thousand feet so we're cut off from the air, at least that's what they think."

The president perked up. "What are you saying? We can beat them from the air?"

"Not quite, Mr. President. We drop down on them from the stratosphere, over four times that height, they'll never see us coming."

Max was intrigued but confused. "We can't bomb them Richard. We start doing that and we risk them sabotaging the canal and retreating."

"No bombs. Sit back and let me explain." The president and vice-president sat back in their chairs and relaxed. Richard continued. "The *PSS Howard Beck* strike group is currently on station a thousand nautical miles from the southern tip of the Baja peninsula. From the flight deck of the *Howard Beck*, we launch seventy-five helium balloons each carrying a small cabin made from reinforced polymers rendering them undetectable by radar. Once all the balloons are launched, the *Howard Beck* will head south to engage the blockade. Each cabin will hold two paratroopers and a deactivated Hal robot - no power signature, no carrier frequency. The cabins have been fitted with small propellers so they can maneuver southbound to the canal. When they're a hundred and twenty thousand feet above the canal, they jump.

Max was shocked. "Christ, Richard, that's over twenty miles straight up. Is that even possible?"

"It's been done a few times. The record is almost a hundred and thirty-six thousand feet. As I was saying, once they jump, they'll be in free fall for over four minutes. When they are a thousand feet above the Canal Zone, they pop their chute and hit the ground."

"Who's looking after the Hal robots on the way down?" asked Max.

"The robots will have self-deploying chutes rigged to altimeters. As soon as the robot drops from the cabin, a drogue parachute will deploy to slow its descent. The paratroopers will hit the ground about thirty seconds before the Hal robots. When they land, they'll basically just look straight up and follow their Hal robot to the ground and collect it. The robots will have reflective patches only seen on infrared. We originally wanted to get Hal on the ground using a tandem jump but the robots weigh too much. The odds of a paratrooper directly attached to a robot actually making it to the ground alive was slim."

The president was optimistic but guarded. "So, you get a hundred and fifty troopers and seventy-five Hal robots on the ground, what comes next?"

The disembodied British accent interrupted, "Mr. President, sir, if I may?"

"What is it, Hal?"

"Even if all the variables are favorable, I estimate that only eighty-six percent of the force will survive the jump."

"Thank you, Hal, noted. Please continue, General."

"Once we are on the ground, our primary objective is to disable communication and radar. Once that is done, the Hal robots can be activated and we secure the three locks."

"Locks?" asked the president.

"Think of them as elevators that raise and lower ships so they can navigate through the canal," said Richard.

"I see, General. Continue."

"While the locks are being secured, the *Howard Beck* will launch an airstrike on the blockade. The airstrike will serve as the perfect distraction while our force on the ground seizes control of the entire canal. Once the canal is secured, the Hal robots join the fight against the blockade and take out any remaining resistance. By the time the *Howard Beck* arrives, she'll be able to navigate the canal from south to north with the rest of our navy bringing up the rear. We finally be able to come over the Rockies while we hit the Chinese from the Gulf of Mexico and the Atlantic. Without reinforcements or supplies and being hit from three sides, we defeat the Chinese inside of six months."

"Fortune favors the bold, General, I'm impressed. What are the risks?"

"Hal?" said Richard.

"Yes, sir, Mr. President. As I've already mentioned, even in optimal conditions, I estimate that only eighty-six percent of the force will survive the jump. Jumping from extreme altitudes in such thin air decreases the amount of friction needed to slow descent. After the first thirty seconds, the paratrooper will reach speeds that will break the sound barrier. While falling at such high speeds, the paratrooper will be in an uncontrolled spin and if he is unable to properly orientate himself, he will lose consciousness. If the weather is not favorable, the balloons could drift during ascent and be unable to maintain course. Also, one of…"

"I get the point, Hal. I'm sure you'll keep us in good hands."

"I most certainly will, Mr. President."

Marshall turned to Richard. "What's your timeframe?"

"We're ready to begin training in the Nevada desert. We'll be ready in two weeks. After that, we're onboard the *Howard Beck* and at the mercy of the weather."

Marshall loved to hear his father's name. The christening of the vessel that bore his father's namesake was one of the proudest moments of his life. He thought of what his father would say and smiled. "Make it so, General."

CHAPTER FIFTEEN

Four days later Richard Dupree was in the Nevada desert looking straight up. "Where is he? I don't see him."

"Seventy-five by three thirty, General." "Thank you, Captain." Richard made the adjustment on the infrared telescope. "Okay, there he is."

"Approaching ninety thousand, General."

"Copy that."

For the purposes of training, the paratrooper was outfitted with an emergency parachute. If the jumper's vital signs indicated he was unconscious, the emergency chute would deploy and bring him safely to the ground. On the actual combat jump, there wouldn't be an emergency chute. Operational security couldn't allow the skies to be filled with visible, open parachutes. Losing consciousness would mean certain death.

"Excellent, he came out of his spin."

"General, with your permission, I'd like to start jumping with the Hal robots."

"Permission granted, Captain. Keep me informed."

"Yes, sir."

Richard patted the young captain on the back and started walking to his truck when he saw Hal jogging toward him. The robot had a rectangular torso with arms and legs but no head. At the center of the robot's torso a red, glowing fish eye lens reminiscent of his science fiction namesake gave a person something to focus on when communicating with it.

"What is it Hal?"

"Sir, I'm speaking to you over your headset." Hal did this when he was within earshot of a person with inadequate security clearance. "I have just received priority communication with one of our deep cover operatives."

"Who?"

"Colonel Theodore Forrest. I'm routing the

message to your tablet."

Richard retrieved his tablet from his jacket pocket, pressed his thumb to the pad and typed in a six-digit code. He read the message three times and still couldn't believe it. "Hal, can you confirm this?"

"I cannot, sir."

"Do you believe it?"

"Sir, I have inadequate data to formulate a working hypothesis. All that we have is the reliability of Colonel Forrest. None of his prior reports have proven to be inaccurate or embellished. Since I have no contradicting data, I recommend that we proceed under the assumption that the report is valid until I can make confirmation."

"This changes everything."

"Yes, sir, I concur. I also recommend that we suspend Operation Miraflores until we receive additional intelligence from Colonel Forrest."

"Absolutely not, Hal."

"Sir, the seventy-five robots assigned to this operation are currently being retrofitted to reduce their overall weight by forty percent. If we receive actionable intelligence from Colonel Forrest, we will not have time to return the robots to full long-range combat readiness."

"The answer is no, Hal, am I clear?"

"Of course you are, sir."

***

Colonel Theodore Forrest was deep behind enemy lines sixty-five miles north of Richmond, Virginia. The journey from the PSA had taken four months. He had slowly made his way across Texas and headed northeast through the Appalachians. He had no identification of any kind and didn't carry a weapon. Once he made it to Virginia, he snuck his way into a labor camp just outside of Quantico. With the basic infrastructure of the region in ruins, the Chinese rounded up Americans by the thousands and forced them into cramped detention centers. The reason for their captivity was twofold; the first being to maintain law and order, the second to carry out the manual labor necessary to keep the Chinese military bases up and running.

Theo had managed to manipulate his way into working inside what he determined to be the headquarters for a major division of the Chinese army. The task actually didn't require much manipulation, no one wanted to work inside the base because they were horribly mistreated and many of them disappeared without a trace. Theo couldn't just outright volunteer for the detail without arousing suspicion. He also had to be careful who he could trust. It was common for his fellow captives to report wrongdoing to the Chinese in exchange for small rewards. All Theo had to do was find a man roughly his age and size that had an intense, deep hatred for the Chinese. Once he had found his man, he traded work details with him and gained access to the base.

Theo spent his days cleaning the latrines in the main headquarters. The enlisted men did not enjoy the luxury of indoor plumbing but instead used portable toilets several hundred yards away from the cluster of buildings. The officers, on the other hand, were far too important and couldn't waste time walking back and forth to the portable toilets. Every floor of the headquarters building had a restroom. Each restroom had three laborers working around the clock keeping it clean and transporting waste away from the building.

Richard Dupree handpicked Theo for this mission because he was fluent in Chinese. None of the Chinese officers had a clue that Theo understood every word they said. Theo was shocked at the amount of intelligence he gathered just from listening. Every day during his twelve-hour shift, a low ranking Chinese officer would fetch Theo and make him clean up the lunch meal and take out the trash. Theo gathered valuable intelligence listening to a dozen officers argue about the war with the PSA.

One particular day the low-ranking Chinese officer burst into the restroom and grabbed Theo by the arm. Theo didn't need to be fluent in Chinese to understand that the junior officer was being chastised by his commanding officer for bringing the wrong bottle of wine. Theo ducked as the wrong bottle smashed on the wall behind him. The junior officer grabbed Theo by the neck and pulled him into the break room. The nervous officer tore through the cabinets and filled Theo's arms with wine glasses. Once the correct bottle was found, the officer kicked Theo in the ass to motivate his journey to the conference room.

The junior officer pantomimed for Theo to collect the dirty wine glasses and replace them with fresh ones. Once Theo nodded his understanding, the junior officer gave Theo the bottle and sat down. Theo pretended to be terrified and allowed his hands to shake as he set about his task so he could take his time and squeeze out a few more seconds in the room. The commanding officer resumed speaking.

"Gentlemen, our primary concern in the next fourteen days will be to begin liberating this territory of its inhabitants so our colonization plans can move forward without issue."

A confused officer raised his hand. "General, do we have the resources for such a task?"

The general did not like being interrupted. "Do our guns not have bullets?" The confused officer looked down at the table and pretended to shuffle some papers. "I asked you a question, Major! Do our guns have bullets?"

"Yes, sir, they do."

"Then use those guns, put bullets in the heads of the American trash still occupying our territory and let their corpses rot where they fall. Or is that too difficult a task for anyone at this table to accomplish?"

No one dared speak.

The general continued, "We have hundreds of millions of our people waiting for their new home to be ready. We cannot afford the luxury of sharing it with the worthless people that were too stupid to evacuate to the PSA. A fitting end to a people that conquered this land and slaughtered the people already living here. Why should we not do the same?"

Theo quietly faded into the background and

slipped out of the conference room unnoticed. At the end of his shift, instead of returning to the detention center, he quickly made his escape. The Chinese didn't bother securing the detention center or monitoring the population. If an American prisoner was found unsupervised away from designated work areas, they were executed on the spot. The corpse was then taken to the detention center and another prisoner was chosen at random to be executed in front of the population. While brutal, the policy was an effective deterrent against prisoners leaving the detention center.

Theo was not worried about getting caught. The Chinese did have random patrols around Quantico but they didn't actively seek out escapees because the Americans really had nowhere to go if they escaped. If an escapee somehow made it off the grounds, they would have to make it across eight hundred miles of Chinese territory to the well-fortified Mississippi River. If by some huge stroke of luck they made it across the river they would then have to travel another eight hundred miles across the barren Great Plains to rejoin their American brethren at the Rocky Mountains. Theo did not have time to make the journey back the Pacific States of America. He had no equipment to broadcast a signal. Even if he did manage to transmit a message, the enemy would zero in on his location and a drone would take him out before he finished.

Theo had to get word to General Dupree immediately. The Chinese would start exterminating every human being that was not of Chinese descent. Time was of the essence and Theo had to think fast.

***

President Marshall Beck was eating breakfast when Hal informed him of General Dupree's arrival and the urgent need to speak with him as fast as humanly possible. Marshall knew something was horribly wrong. The general had a strict timetable to prepare for Operation Miraflores and his sudden arrival from the Nevada desert had him concerned. He stepped off the elevator at the command level to find Richard waiting for him.

"Richard! What the hell is going on?"

"Mr. President, please," Richard raised his arm in the direction of the command center. Marshall nodded his head and the two walked toward the outer door of the command center. Hal opened the door and once inside, Richard waited for the door to secure before speaking.

"Mr. President, I've just received a deeply disturbing message from Colonel Forrest and we have little time to react. Here it is." Richard called up the message on his tablet and gave it to the president. The message was short but powerful.

MASS EXTERMINATION TO BEGIN.
COLONIZATION IMMINENT.

"Have you confirmed this, General?"

"No, Mr. President. We are not in contact with Colonel Forrest."

"How did you get this message?"

"Theo is nothing short of a genius. He sent this message using Morse code."

"Morse code?"

"Yes, Mr. President. Hal intercepted the message from a reconnaissance satellite. Theo managed to get his hands on a high powered spotlight at an abandoned airfield."

"Are you telling me the colonel gave his life to get us this message? The Chinese aren't blind, they must have spotted it."

"The Chinese didn't see a thing. The colonel spent upwards of an hour to relay the message, one letter at a time. He repeated the message six times before the sun came up."

"And you know it's from him?

"Yes, Mr. President. His authentication code preceded each message."

"Do we have any way to extract Colonel Forrest

and get more intel from him?"

"No, Mr. President, he's on his own. Theo's one of our best, he'll make it back."

Marshall slumped down in his chair, defeated. "This changes everything. We cannot sit idly by while the Chinese slaughter our people and make our land their own. They hold the line at the Mississippi and if we come charging over the Rockies the war will be over. They outnumber us three to one and have enough firepower to wipe us out before we could get half way across the Great Plains. What the hell are we going to do, Richard?"

"Mr. President, how quickly can the vice president be here?"

"Hal?"

"Yes, Mr. President. I have informed Vice President Harris and he will depart Seattle in the next ten minutes."

CHAPTER SIXTEEN

Vice President Maxwell Harris was aboard Air Force Two en route to Beck Castle. He had departed Seattle four hours ahead of schedule, which suited him just fine. His sudden departure meant he could cancel a long string of boring meetings. While he was content to leave behind his fake smiles, he was concerned that the president had recalled him so abruptly. Max was well aware that the bulk of his duties as the vice president was to serve as a buffer for his boss. Everyone wanted the president's ear for all manners of triviality and most were content to spend ten minutes with Max.

"Okay, Hal, we're in the air. Tell me what's going on."

"Yes, sir. Direct your attention to the main screen."

Max looked at the brief report detailing Theo's message. "Hal, is that it?"

"Unfortunately, it is, sir."

"Really wish we had more to go on. What's the plan?"

"Sir, at the request of the president, I am still attempting to accumulate more definitive intelligence so that an operation with favorable odds of success can be carried out."

"Hal, I'm sure you are. Any luck?"

"Sir, I am currently examining and comparing vast amounts of information to confirm the report sent by Colonel Forrest. I will present my findings to you, the president, and General Dupree shortly after we land."

"Fair enough. What is my wife up to?"

"Sir, Mrs. Harris and the First Lady are in San Fransisco for the reopening of the Golden Gate Bridge."

"Now that's a PR trip I would have actually enjoyed."

"Sir, your wife is much more attractive than you."

"You're getting funnier, Hal."

"Thank you, sir. I have been making an effort."

"Howard would be proud."

"Yes, sir, I know he would."

Max paused for a moment and a small glimmer of a smile cracked through his pain induced scowl. He wasn't sure if Hal's reply carried with it a bit of sadness or if he was merely projecting his own. Could the artificial intelligence long for the company of his deceased creator? Howard always viewed his relationship with Hal as father and son. Did Hal consider himself as having lost a father? Did he miss him?

"I take it Chrissy Dupree is with my son?"

"Yes, sir, that is correct. Would you like to speak to her?"

Max was about to say yes but thought better of it. Richard Dupree's sixteen-year-old daughter was a mature, competent babysitter. His little boy was in good hands. "No, it can wait. I'll check on them later today."

"Very good, sir."

Max spent the rest of the flight trying to calm his nerves. His battle with chronic pain had its ups and downs. Being medicated brought with it a hazy fog that the vice president tried to avoid. On the other hand, the pain made him angry and bitter, a combination that was not suited for politics. The only thing he could do was find a middle ground. Over the counter pain medication was weak, but it dulled the horrific pain enough for him the function. In his current state, however, he would normally admit defeat and indulge in narcotics. Given what was at stake with Colonel Forrest's report, he needed a clear and focused mind. He would have to settle with his cane.

Max exited Air Force Two and slowly made his way to the elevator that would take him far beneath the surface to Beck Castle. Once on the command level, he walked the long corridor to the command center and was pleased that he did not have to wait outside the outer door. Richard Dupree was waiting just inside.

"Max! Glad you could join us. How was your flight?"

"It was fine. How's Nevada?"

"Hot."

Max sat down in front of the ten-foot high spherical monitor. Formal etiquette dictated that is was highly disrespectful to sit down before the president and even more so to not shake his hand before taking your seat. Max would never do this in public and Marshall Beck didn't really mind. He hated being coddled and fussed over just as much as his father did when he was alive. In the company of friends, he enjoyed being treated a normal person.

The president didn't waste time. "Hal? What have you got for us?"

A map of the Chinese-American territory zoomed into view in front of them. "Gentlemen, after careful review of the data at hand, I have surmised that Colonel Forrest's report holds merit. Reviewing images from reconnaissance satellites over the past eleven days has shown something out of the ordinary. While it does not confirm Colonel Forrest's report, it does indicate that something of significance is taking place."

Richard interrupted, "Elaborate, please."

"Yes, General. I have compared the movements of the population of the Chinese-American territory prior to Colonel Forrest's report with the movement taking place afterwards."

Now Max was the one interrupting, "Wait. What do you mean 'population?' Are you saying you've tracked the movements every living person in the territory since the occupation?"

"Yes, sir, I have to the best of my ability. The task was quite monumental in its undertaking. My original estimates for completion were over fourteen hours. I applied a set of algorithms …"

"We get the point, Hal," said Max, "What did you find?"

"Yes, sir, as you know, there are currently ninety-three labor camps holding just under a million prisoners. The Chinese utilize the prisoners to carry out various labor-intensive tasks. On any given day, between twenty-two and fifty-three percent of the prison population are taken from the camps to perform labor. However, for reasons unknown, on some days that figure is as low as three percent."

"Hal, I don't like 'for reasons unknown,' at least give us a guess," said the president.

"Yes, Mr. President. Likely scenarios could be security related, to perform a census in order to locate particular prisoners for interrogation. Another possibility would be for health concerns, to stop the spread of disease."

"Thank you, Hal, continue," said the president.

"You are welcome, Mr. President. Gentlemen, the one factor that has not changed since the occupation is that days of extremely low prisoner movement have never exceeded a twenty-four hour period. Normal operations have always proceeded at sunrise of the following day."

General Dupree, the ever-vigilant tactician, was the first to figure it out. "That changed for the first time after Theo's report."

"Yes, General Dupree, you are indeed correct. When Colonel Forrest sent his report, prisoner movement at the labor camps was already down to one percent. This occurred yesterday. Today, prisoner movement has remained at one percent."

The president took a deep breath. "Hal, are you saying the mass extermination has already begun?"

"Mr. President, I do not believe that to be correct. The labor camps have remained secured, both inside and out, for thirty-seven hours. I have not observed a large military presence at the labor camps to carry out executions on a large scale. Such an undertaking would also require the disposal of corpses, which I have not yet seen."

"Thank god for that," said Richard.

"Gentlemen, I am afraid that is only half of my report. In regards to the rest of the American population in Chinese territory, I have also noted a radical change in movement patterns. When the labor camps were secured, the scattered communities of Americans were also restricted in their movement."

"How is that significant?" asked Richard, "It's not

like they're allowed to move around that much in the first place."

"That is correct, General, however, the Chinese military are not allowing Americans to leave their homes for any reason. Examples were quickly made of those not wishing to comply with the mandate. In less than twelve hours, every American community has shown little to no movement. It is evident that the Chinese are preparing for something on a large scale. Colonel Forrest's report would appear to be valid. Gentlemen, that concludes my report."

"Simon Sterling strikes again."

Max and Richard exchanged puzzled glances. Richard broke the silence. "Mr. President?"

"The piece of shit that assassinated President Powers and wiped his ass with the Constitution? One of the first things he did when founded the Unified American Empire was to confiscate every firearm from every civilian. If our brothers and sisters on the other side of the Mississippi had the means to resist, the outcome of this war would be entirely different. Hal, what about colonization? Have the Chinese started moving their citizens?"

"Mr. President, I do not have adequate satellite coverage of the Asian continent to make such a determination. I could reassign the satellite network, however, it would impair my ability to monitor either the North American continent or the Empire of Iran's conquest of Europe."

"No desire to do that, Hal. Don't change a thing."

"Of course, sir."

Marshall turned to Richard. "General, please tell me you have something that resembles a plan."

"Mr. President, the plan is already in motion. Our plan to retake the Panama Canal can be adapted to secure the Mississippi. If we can disable their defenses along the river we can finally come over the Rockies and bring the fight to their front door. Worst-case scenario, we fail to secure the river but it would still delay their plans for mass extermination, basically just buy us more time. If we succeed and secure the river, we keep pushing east and liberate our people along the way. It's just crazy enough to work. They won't know what hit 'em. Hal, what do you think?"

"General, the odds of success are dramatically lower compared to Operation Miraflores. I do concur, however, that any such operation focused on the Mississippi River will serve as a distraction to their plans of mass extermination. If the president authorizes such a plan, the plan will need to be executed in the next eighteen hours, prior to sunrise on the East Coast."

"Mr. President?" said Richard.

"I'm not convinced just yet, Max, you've been quiet, what do you think?"

"Mr. President, I realize the need for immediate action is present, millions of lives depend on it. I just can't stop thinking about the bigger picture. Why such a bold move? The Chinese are so desperate to colonize the East Coast that they are willing to join the ranks of the Third Reich with their own American Holocaust? What are they going through that is so bad that would make them do such a thing? They've got us trapped on our side of the Rockies, powerless to fight them. Why provoke us? They know that slaughtering Americans by the millions would elicit a swift response from us. I just can't figure out why and it's bothering me."

The president paused and contemplated Max's words. "I agree. Whatever the reason, we still have to do everything in our power to stop them. I'm sure their motives will be made clear soon enough. We'll cross that bridge when we get to it. Maxwell, I need you in the here and now. What do you think?"

"Richard knows what he's doing, I trust him."

Marshall stood and paced back and forth, deep in thought. "General, you have my authorization to carry out this operation. You and Hal iron out the details and have it to me it ninety minutes. Make it a good one, General, win or lose, the Battle of the Mississippi is going to end the war."

CHAPTER SEVENTEEN

Eighty-two minutes later General Richard Dupree was back in the command center with the president and vice-president. Richard did not take his seat and paced around the room as he spoke.

"Mr. President, I want to stress to both of you that we are gambling our entire military force on this operation. Everything we have, right down to the last bullet will be used to stop the enemy. Even then it might not be enough, but we have to try. Far too many lives are at stake for us to be conservative in our efforts." Richard paused, realizing that his anger was interfering with his duties. He composed himself and continued. "For the last six months, we've been in a stalemate. The Chinese have planted roots along the Mississippi, digging in deep and fortifying their lines. We've been licking our wounds and barely holding the line at the Rockies, just praying the Chinese won't realize how vulnerable we truly are. For the time being, they don't seem to have any interest in engaging us and we don't have the means to bring the fight to them without being slaughtered. They have the luxury of eight hundred miles of wide open space to see us coming and they know it."

The president smiled. "That's where Operation Miraflores comes in."

"Exactly," said Richard, "our plans to capture the Panama Canal can be modified to take the Mississippi. I've designated it Operation Nantucket."

"Catchy title," said Max. "A symbol of our destination just beyond the shores of the Atlantic."

"You really think seventy-five helium balloons is enough? The Chinese have three major military installations along the river," said President Beck.

"And those three installations will be our targets. We have the balloons, Mr. President. The Panama Canal is a much smaller target and seventy-five teams was sufficient for the task. We have the manpower and resources for three hundred balloons giving us six hundred paratroopers and three hundred Hal robots. We focus our airborne assaults on Minneapolis, St. Louis, and Baton Rouge, a hundred teams each. Those three installations are responsible for their long-range radar, communications, and most importantly - the bulk of their air defense. We hit all three simultaneously and take out their communications and radar, then we're clear to hit them with everything we've got. Once we break through enemy lines, we airdrop weapons, ammo, and paratroopers to as many American settlements and prison camps as we can, giving them a fighting chance to defend themselves. Then we fight like hell on the ground and scoop them up along the way. We don't stop until we get to the Atlantic." Richard stopped pacing and faced Marshall and Max, ready to answer questions.

"That's it? You make it sound so easy," said Max.

"Knock it off, you grumpy bastard, you're not helping," said the president. "General, I trust we can accomplish the mission in the time allotted?"

"Yes, Mr. President. The logistical side of things are greatly in our favor. The bulk of our military force is protecting the line at the Rockies. To put it in the simplest of terms, we give the order to haul ass towards the Mississippi and keep going. Our timetable will be cutting it close. We have to gut the Hal robots so they're light enough for the trip. Hal estimates it will take about six hours to get that done. We barely have enough time to get one training jump in for the paratroopers we're adding to the mission. The operation will commence four hours before sunrise on the East Coast."

"The plan sounds solid, what are the risks?" asked Max.

Richard paused for second. "Hal? You wanna take that one?"

"Of course, General. Gentlemen, the most daunting obstacle we are facing is the weather. Right now, weather conditions are favorable. However, should those conditions change, it could prove difficult keeping our paratroopers on target. We are also lacking in crucial Chinese intelligence. They have gone to great lengths to mask their operations and I am unable to decrypt their communications."

"We're not going in blind, are we Hal?" asked the president.

"No, Mr. President, I still have satellite reconnaissance across all visible spectrums. For Operation Miraflores, I estimated that eighty-six percent of the paratroopers would survive the jump. Given that seventy-five percent of the paratroopers will only have one training jump prior to the mission, my current estimate is that seventy-one percent of the paratroopers will survive the fall. If we lack sufficient manpower at one of the targets and can not disable long range radar and communications, the operation will fail and our assault force will be destroyed long before it arrives at the Mississippi River."

The three men sat in silence for a brief moment, contemplating Hal's dire estimation. "You know what I just realized?" said Max, "We've never known exactly how many Americans are behind enemy lines. Hal?"

"Yes, sir, the current American population in Chinese territory is between twelve point one and twelve point two million people."

"That's it?" said Richard.

"I am afraid so, sir. The bulk of the American population east of the Mississippi River evacuated to the PSA in the early days of the war. Once the Chinese fortified the Mississippi, any American still in the territory was essentially trapped. Since the Chinese do not waste any of their infrastructure on American refugees outside of the prison camps, the Americans have had to provide for themselves. A combination of starvation, disease, and lawlessness has diminished the American population to the current estimate."

"Christ, I thought it was at least twice that," said Max.

"Regardless the figure," said the president, "we still have an obligation to save as many lives as we can before the Chinese start murdering them. We do not have the luxury of time to plan the perfect operation, we have no choice but to do our best with what little time we have."

"Yes, Mr. President, but I will say it again - I'm terrified of the reason why the Chinese are doing this. What the hell is going on that would make them do something so horrific? They must have a reason."

"I'm sure we'll know soon enough," said the president. "General Dupree, Godspeed to you, sir." The president stood and walked the two men to the door of the command center. "I will remain here in the command center monitoring the operation. Maxwell, in the interest of continuity of government, I think it is prudent that you and I do not share the same space until this is over. Why don't you head to San Francisco and join your wife? Hal can keep you updated on the operation."

Max cracked a smile. "If I have to, Mr. President."

***

Max and Richard exited the elevator and walked down the corridor to Max's quarters. The sensors in the hallway recognized Max and opened the door before he got there. Max headed for the kitchen and Richard walked into the living room.

Max poured cranberry juice in a glass and added vodka. "Want a drink?"

"No, I'm good."

Chrissy Dupree entered the living room from an adjacent hallway and ran to her father, wrapping her arms around him. "Dad! Didn't think I'd get to see you!"

Richard kissed the top of his daughter's head. "Can't stay, baby, I'm about to leave. Just wanted to see you and your brother before I left."

Chrissy stepped back and turned her head to the hallway. "Tommy! Your dad's here!" She turned back to face her father. "You should probably just leave him alone for now. He's still pissed at you."

Richard didn't get a chance to answer. Max's son, Thomas, came screaming down the hallway. "Daddy! You're home! I'm watching *Iron Man*, wanna watch with me?"

"Sorry, buddy, I'm headed out in a few minutes to

join your mom."

"Can I come? Please?"

"Can't do it, pal. You stay here with Chrissy and your mom and I will be back soon. Tell you what, I can use some help packing, wanna give me a hand? Come on." Max headed to his bedroom with his son.

Richard smiled at the sight of his friend interacting with his son. Max was in a foul mood most of the time, but when he was with his son, his bitterness was replaced with joy. Richard then thought of his own son and looked at his daughter. "So, he's still pissed at me?"

Chrissy nodded her head. "Yep, don't think he's gonna change his mind anytime soon."

"Plenty of things your brother can do besides join the military."

"Dad, he doesn't want to do anything else. He's twenty years old, he's an adult that can make his own decisions."

"I know that. But as long as I have anything to say about it, he's not joining the military, not while I'm the highest-ranking officer. Trust me, he'll get over it."

"Okay, I'll try and talk to him, but once he cools down, you need to work this out."

Richard was confident that the problems he was having with his son would smooth over soon enough. By this time tomorrow, there would either be no war to fight or no military for his son to join.

CHAPTER EIGHTEEN

"General Dupree, with all due respect, sir, I'm asking you to please reconsider." Colonel Mark Samson knew he was on thin ice but felt it was his duty to help the general see reason.

"Are you volunteering to take my place, Colonel?"

"No, sir, I simply think the prudent course of action would be for you to oversee the operation from a safer environment."

"Colonel Samson, do you feel unfit to carry out your orders?" Richard was standing on a stool while technicians attached an oxygen tank to his flight suit.

"Not at all, sir, I just think you're taking an unnecessary risk."

"Colonel, your objections are noted. This operation is in desperate need of qualified paratroopers. I'm a qualified paratrooper and my skills are needed, it's as simple as that."

"But sir, surely we have someone that can take your place. We need you here."

"Colonel, I'm not about to sit this one out while a less experienced jumper puts his life on the line. Did you really think I was gonna sit this one out?"

The colonel grinned, "Not really, sir."

"Mark, you know as well as I do that any well thought out plan goes to complete shit the moment it's executed. I need to be on the front lines where I belong."

"Yes sir, General. You know someone had to at least try."

"Colonel, I'd expect nothing less. You ready for this?"

"Yes, sir."

"Don't sweat it, you've got the easy job. When the time is right, all you gotta do is light a fire under everyone's ass and send 'em my way."

"General, I think it's a bit more complicated than that. There hasn't been a battle of this magnitude since Normandy."

"The Allies didn't have Hal during World War II."

"True, but the Allies had more than a day to plan the invasion of France."

"Colonel, I'd give my right arm to have just a week to plan this operation, but the Chinese are going to start exterminating twelve million Americans very soon. If we waited another week there's no telling how many of our people would be murdered." Richard raised his arms to allow the technicians to double check his harness.

"You really think two hundred troopers and a hundred Hal robots can cripple a Chinese military base?"

"Colonel, I absolutely guarantee you that those three Chinese bases will not be operational. We will take the Mississippi, I promise you that." Richard extended his arm and the two officers shook hands.

***

Two hours earlier Richard was sitting in a conference room staring at the wall. He had just briefed the commanding officers of the other two jumps. He was confident they would succeed in conquering the Chinese bases at Minneapolis and Baton Rouge while he did the same in St. Louis. Richard knew both men well and didn't hesitate to put his full faith in them but one factor still bothered him a great deal - the odds.

"Hal?"

"Yes, sir."

"Please tell me the odds on the combat jumps have improved."

"They have, sir. The closer we get to the jump we have a more accurate picture of weather patterns. I can also incorporate the results of the training jump and maintenance reports of the crew cabins to arrive at a new estimation. I can now calculate that seventy-nine percent of the paratroopers will survive the jump."

"Those are still shitty odds. If one of the three targets suffers more than a ten percent loss, the operation will be next to impossible to pull off."

"I concur, sir."

"How long will each team have to carry out their

mission?"

"Sir, the first priority of each team will be to disable the communication tower so the Chinese can not call for help. After that, the Hal robots can be activated. The Hal robots should be able to accomplish the mission in under sixty seconds. However, the greatest risk to the operation will be the air traffic control towers. Since I am unable to calculate with any degree of certainty where each team will land, we stand the risk of a team landing on or near the airfield and being seen by the air traffic control towers. Such an error will result in complete failure."

"The entire mission can end up in the shitter before we even hit the ground."

"Correct, sir."

"Okay, let's say we succeed and bring down all three bases. How long before the Chinese realize three of their bases have gone dark and react with force?"

"Sir, it is highly unlikely the Chinese will resort to military action without confirming the cause. The prudent course of action will be to send drones from nearby bases to obtain visual confirmation. I will endeavor to engage and destroy any approaching drone before it reaches the target. Such an engagement will, however, only delay a military reaction for a short period of time."

Richard slumped down in his chair and rubbed his temples. "Okay, so how long?"

"Sir, a conservative estimate would be twenty to twenty-five minutes."

"Jesus Christ, this has got to be the most foolhardy operation in the history of war. A month wouldn't be long enough to prepare and we're stupid enough to think we can do it in a day. I really wish Howard was here, he would know what to do."

"Sir, with respect to my creator, I can assure you that is not correct."

Richard sat up straight and took a few seconds to respond. "What?"

"Sir, have you never wondered why when Howard died he gave full operational control of my systems to you and not his son?"

Richard sunk back down in his chair and sighed. "I always thought it was because he died in my arms."

"No sir, from the moment I was created Howard designated a guardian to be responsible for my program in the event of his death. His wife Meredith was the first to fill the role. Upon her death, the responsibility was passed to Dr. Sebastian Biggs. Are you familiar with Dr. Biggs, sir?"

"No."

"Dr. Biggs was one of the co-founders of Beck Enterprises. He later resigned to assume the position of NASA Administrator. After the Collapse of 2027, Dr. Biggs went missing and Howard assigned guardianship of my program to his son Marshall."

"What changed his mind? Why'd he pick me over his own son?"

"Sir, Howard came to hold you in very high regard. While he found his son more than capable, he regarded you as a military genius and felt your skills and experience made you the better choice."

"How did Marshall take the news?"

"Sir, Howard never informed anyone that they had been selected as my guardian."

"I don't know what to say, Hal. This is a lot to take in. Why haven't you ever told me this?"

"Sir, Howard never directly instructed me to keep the information confidential, but since he never told anyone I felt it was best to honor the spirit of his decision."

"What made you change your mind?"

"Sir, I felt you needed a boost in confidence. If Howard were here now, he'd be asking you what to do."

Richard thought of his dearly departed friend and wiped a tear from his eye. "The most brilliant mind of our time thought I was a genius, that's high praise coming from him. I just have this gnawing feeling that I'm about to let him down."

"Sir, you know I will do everything in my power to make Howard proud of us."

Richard sat up, a gleam in his eye. He was on his

feet, pacing back and forth down the length of the room. "That's it, Hal! I think you may have just solved our problem."

"Sir, I am afraid you will need to elaborate."

"Hal, tell me about the power cells in your robots."

CHAPTER NINETEEN

General Richard Dupree was crammed inside a small cabin with another paratrooper and a boxy looking contraption that was a modified Hal robot. He couldn't move his torso or legs more than a half an inch and the fact that his arms were folded across his chest made him feel like he was trapped inside a coffin.

"Hal, open the comm channel."

"Yes, sir, you are broadcasting."

"If I may have your attention, this is General Dupree. Ladies and gentlemen, I want to thank each and every one of you for embarking on the most daring mission every conceived. I wish we had more time to prepare for this mission, but we all know what's at stake. Millions of lives hang in the balance. I know you have all been briefed on what's about to happen, but I think it is wise to go over the details one last time. It's important that you commit these details to memory because once we're airborne; the Chinese will sever all communications to avoid early detection. That also means that we won't have computer support, we gotta do this the old fashioned way - by looking at the simple gauges in front of us. It will take us over two hours to reach the correct altitude and another two hours to reach our respective drop zones. That means you need to keep an eye on the gauges and use your propellers to stay on course. You won't do us any good if you end up fifty miles from the target. When you jump, a short ripcord will drop the Hal robots out of the bottom of the cabin. The first thirty seconds will be crucial; chances are high that you'll be spinning wildly out of control. If you are unable to correct your descent, you will lose consciousness and that will be the end of you. Once you're in a stable descent, you'll be heading straight down for four minutes. When you're a thousand feet above the DZ, your chute will open and it will be a very rough landing. You'll have a few seconds at best to brace yourself. If you end up with a broken leg or even a sprained ankle, you'll serve little purpose to the mission, so make sure you nail the landing.

You all know your primary, secondary, and tertiary targets. Whoever takes out the communication tower, switch on your Hal robot so he can power up his friends. If all hell breaks loose before the comm tower goes down, switch on the Hal robots and our friend will lay waste to the airfield and hopefully give our invasion force a better chance. Godspeed to us all."

"Sir, the channel is closed. All of my robots except for this one have been deactivated."

"Thank you, Hal."

"Sir, before I power down this robot and sever communication, may I ask a question?"

"Of course, what is it?"

"Sir, I am concerned that you have not shared the full details of Operation Nantucket in it's entirety."

"You really think everyone involved in this operation needs to know every last detail?"

"No sir, I do not."

"Then what's the problem, Hal?"

"Sir, you misunderstand me, I am concerned that you have not shared all of the details of Operation Nantucket with the president or vice-president."

"I understand your concerns, Hal. I'm not changing my mind on this and you are to keep the information to yourself like we discussed. Is that going to be a problem?"

"No sir, it will not. You are the sole administrator of my program, I am unable to disobey your commands."

"Good. Anything else?"

"No, sir."

"Power down my friend. I'll see you on the ground."

***

Richard had performed many HALO jumps during his military career as a Navy SEAL. He had never been afraid of heights and jumping from above the clouds didn't bother him at all. This jump was so far above his level of experience that it might as well have been his first. He was currently in the neighborhood of twenty miles straight up, over four times the height of a standard HALO jump. Since the Chinese had the airspace above the Mississippi River locked down tight this radical move was necessary to strike without being seen. The previous four hours of the trip had been filled with fear and doubt and Richard hated every minute of it. The more he thought about it, he was certain the last minute insurance policy he had in place would need to be used.

Richard reversed the propellers attached to the cabin to stop the balloon's forward movement. He looked at the gauges in front of him and tried his best to trust them. These gauges were commonplace during World War II almost a century ago, but to Richard they felt far too simple to be effective. The fact that he had to plot the course and make corrections with pencil and paper made him very nervous.

"General Dupree, sir! Look!"

Richard could barely hear the man sitting directly behind him. Lieutenant Banaski was shouting through his helmet. Richard moved his feet apart to get a better view of the plexiglass trap door beneath him. The seat he was strapped into was angled slightly forward so he could see down. "I see it, Lieutenant! That's a good sign! Just what we wanted to see! It's beautiful!" Richard looked down in the darkness and could see the mighty Mississippi River shimmering in all her glory. It was a sight to behold in the darkness; he could only imagine what she looked like in the daylight.

Richard looked to his left and right and counted four other cabins relatively level to his own. He flipped a switch in front of him. "Hit your light, Lieutenant!"

"Copy that, sir! Done!"

On the port and starboard sides of the cabin, a strobe light began emitting three pulses in rapid succession. Richard's field of vision was limited, but he could see lights on dozens of cabins spread out of what he hoped was about a square mile.

"Lieutenant! You ready for his?"

"Not a chance in hell, sir!"

"Me neither, here we go!" Richard reached up

with both hands and pulled down the lever above his head that opened the trap door beneath him. He heard his safety harness snap open and his seat slowly pitched forward. He carefully planted his feet on the rail and grabbed the bar above him and raised himself up. He paused for only a brief second to ensure his footing, leaned forward, and stepped off the rail.

Richard was shocked at how quickly he accelerated. He knew the air was much thinner and provided practically no resistance against his two hundred pound body. He wasn't sure but he was almost certain that for a brief second he could see the curvature of the earth on both the east and west sides. The sheer magnitude of what he had just seen both amazed and horrified him. The first ten seconds of the jump were going smoothly until he made the crucial error of turning his head to the right to find nothing but the blackness of space. He tried to look at the ground and battled the sensation that he was veering off into the cold vacuum of nothingness. Richard's fears were intensified as his body tumbled violently. His vision was a rapid blur of confusing shapes and varying degrees of light and dark. Richard instinctively reached up for his ripcord to end this madness only to be reminded that it would be worthless until he was two thousand feet above ground level, a measure he implemented to insure the skies wouldn't be filled with clearly visible parachutes.

What have I done? No one can survive this. Every single jumper is falling to their death.

Richard no longer had any sense of orientation. He rolled over on his back and remained there for five seconds staring at blackness. Richard had never felt such terror in his life. He glanced at his biometric readout and saw his blood pressure was 180/120 and his pulse was 190. He knew he had to calm down or he would have a stroke.

I'm getting light-headed. I'm going to pass out and this will all be over.

Richard raised his arms and tried to change his orientation so he could see the ground and thankfully it worked, or at least he thought it worked but didn't really care one way or the other. He'd rather be looking at the spinning ground than the terror of staring into the abyss. With his view much improved, he could tell that the spin had slowed but not enough to make a difference. He quickly glanced at the biometric readout to find his vitals still dangerously high.

Richard closed his fingers and cautiously cupped his hands. His spin slowed considerably but he was still nowhere near being in control. He guessed that he had been in a spin for about thirty seconds and knew he would not survive much longer.

I'm about to die.

In his last seconds of consciousness, Richard decided that he wasn't just going to give up and die without a fight. He looked to the ground and focused on a string of lights that he assumed was the landing field at the St. Louis base. The string of lights came into and out of his field of vision twice. On the third time around, he tucked his arms to his side and lurched his body at a downward angle like a missile. At seven hundred miles an hour, the maneuver would either correct his spin or tumble him head over feet and snap his spine like a twig. Seconds away from losing consciousness, he didn't have much of a choice but to try.

Holy shit, that worked. Breathe, breathe!

Richard was finally in a stable descent and the g-forces slamming his body finally became manageable. The light-headedness faded and he was pleased to see his vitals were in the safe zone. He checked the altimeter and was shocked to see he was already halfway to the ground. Richard welcomed the comforting embrace of much thicker air and could feel himself slowing down. With nothing but ground in his field of vision he enabled the infrared feature on his visor. It took a few seconds for Richard to comprehend what he was seeing. The easiest feature to place was the landing strip on the airfield. Once he had done that, the rest of the installation was easy enough to plot out in his mind. Richard looked at the altimeter to find he was four thousand feet above ground level. In the span of a few seconds, Richard determined, much to his surprise, that he was going to land inside of his designated drop zone, roughly a quarter of a mile from the airfield.

When the altimeter registered a thousand feet above ground level, the parachute deployed and Richard quickly went from terminal velocity to ten miles an hour in a matter of seconds. A few seconds after that, he was on solid ground.

Richard was disoriented for a few seconds and then remembered he had to collect his Hal robot. He looked straight up and with the aide of his visor's infrared capabilities; he spotted the faint reflective patches fixed in various places to the shell of the robot. The reflective patches didn't register with the naked eye, but in infrared, they lit up quite well. Richard detached his parachute as he walked and once free, jogged the short distance to where the disabled robot had landed. When he arrived, he noticed Lieutenant Banaski was already there.

"Sir, that was one hell of jump, wasn't it? I was spinning hard for a few seconds there, scared the shit out of me. You?"

Richard stared at the young lieutenant for a second in disbelief. *A few seconds? Are you kidding me?* "Focus, Lieutenant, we've got a job to do."

"Yes, sir. Sorry, sir."

Richard looked down at his lifeless friend. "Wheel on your side good?" Richard knelt down and checked the small wheel on his side of the disabled robot.

"Mine's good."

"Let's get moving," said Richard.

The two men hoisted the rectangular contraption at a forty-five degree angle and wheeled him along the ground like they were casually strolling through an airport terminal with a three hundred pound suitcase.

The two men were startled by a loud thud ten yards away that kicked up a cloud of dirt. They dropped the robot and hit the ground, certain the Chinese were lobbing mortar rounds on top of them. Richard slowly raised his head from the dirt and saw a bloody finger a few inches from his face. "Get up, Lieutenant, we're fine."

"What the hell was that, sir?"

"One of our brothers didn't make it." Richard stood up and walked the short distance to the mangled corpse. The body was horribly contorted, all four limbs had been broken in several places and his head had nearly decapitated from its torso. Richard closed his eyes for a few seconds, swallowing the guilt that would otherwise consume him. "Let's go."

"Sir, shouldn't we—"

"Nothing we can do, Lieutenant, we have a job to do." Richard knelt down and grabbed his side of the robot. "Now, Lieutenant."

"Yes sir." Lieutenant Banaski took his place opposite of Richard the two men continued to the airfield. Along the way, they came upon three more corpses like the one that crash-landed next to them. Richard hoped the four dead paratroopers had been the only casualties from the jump but knew better; this idiotic plan was headed towards failure. The two officers traversed the quarter mile to the outskirts of the airfield. The floodlights illuminating the perimeter extended about a hundred yards into the darkness and Richard stopped fifty yards shy of the floodlights' reach.

"Now we wait, Lieutenant. Whoever takes out the comm tower will activate the Hal robots. All we have to do is wait for our friend here to …"

Alarm sirens shrieked. Stadium lights lit up the darkness and turned night into day. Powerful strobe lights flickered atop buildings. Chinese soldiers were moving all over the base. Screaming and gunfire could be heard in multiple locations. Richard grabbed Lieutenant Banaski's arm and pulled him to the ground. "Get the fuck down!"

"Oh Jesus, we're fucked!" screamed the lieutenant. "What the fuck are we gonna do now?"

"Calm down, son, this will all be over very soon." Richard was certain someone would have activated Hal by now but didn't wait to find out. He ran his hand down the side of the robot and was about to pull up a panel that exposed the on switch when the robot activated. The legs folded down and two arms clicked out and locked into place. The red fish eye lens in the center of the robot glowed. "Hal, initiate the failsafe, you—."

The robot did not acknowledge General Dupree and was already airborne before Richard could finish his sentence. Richard lifted the frightened lieutenant to his feet. Banaski started toward the airfield when Richard grabbed his arm.

"Stop! Follow me!" Richard sprinted away from the airfield. Banaski looked over his shoulder at the airfield and back at his commanding officer. Richard did not slow down and screamed over his shoulder. "Now, Lieutenant! Get your ass moving!"

Banaski started jogging. "Sir! Sir! You're going the wrong way!"

Richard was furious and screamed, "Run! Run! Run!"

Banaski felt the desperation in General Dupree's screams and it finally dawned on him what was about to happen. The young lieutenant had never run so fast in his entire life.

CHAPTER TWENTY

Nine hundred and twelve yards away from General Dupree, a mortally wounded paratrooper activated the first Hal robot. The dying man lifted the panel with the two remaining fingers on his left hand and flipped the switch. In the span of a few picoseconds, Hal activated the other ninety-nine robots assigned to the mission and gathered the critical data he needed for the mission. Another few picoseconds elapsed and he had a clear picture of what was transpiring.

No data could be gathered from the missions taking place at Minneapolis and Baton Rouge, meaning the Hal robots had not yet been activated. Twenty-three paratroopers assigned to the St. Louis mission did not survive the fall. Another twenty paratroopers missed the drop zone and could not contribute to the mission. The closest was six point two miles away and the furthest was forty-seven point nine miles away. Of the fifty-seven paratroopers that successfully landed in the drop zone, nineteen were now deceased. Three point two seconds prior to his activation; the Chinese had sounded the general alarm. At the time of his activation, Hal detected eight radio transmissions from the Chinese seeking clarification as to why the alarm had been sounded. No outgoing transmissions had been detected. No order had been given to the airfield to launch any craft. Hal concluded that none of the mission objectives would be completed before the Chinese sent a distress signal. The thirty-eight remaining paratroopers were now facing active resistance. Even in optimal conditions, the robots in the combat zone would not be able to disable communication in the fleeting seconds remaining. If a distress call went out, the Chinese would be on full alert and the invasion force getting under way from the Rockies would be annihilated. General Dupree had given Hal clear instructions on what to do in this circumstance. Operation Nantucket was about to go down in flames. Hal initiated the failsafe order.

The robot closest to the airfield was the one

assigned to General Dupree. Hal activated it sent it hurtling to the airfield; no time could be allotted to converse with the general. Hal disengaged the safety lock to the robot's power cell and activated the detonation command. The small nuclear power cell went critical three hundred and nine feet above the airfield and detonated. The kiloton blast carved out a crater sixty feet across and sent out a blast wave that leveled every building within a two thousand foot radius. The fighter jets on the airfield scattered through the air like toys.

Three nanoseconds after the first detonation, a second robot's power cell went critical five hundred and seventeen feet above the center of the Chinese base. When the blast waves from both explosions subsided, nothing remained of the Chinese base. Thousands had died, including the majority of the paratroopers that had dropped from the stratosphere.

Hal immediately dispatched the functioning robots to collect the surviving paratroopers. A robot landed on the ground next to Richard Dupree. "Sir, are you injured?"

Richard was lying in the dirt. After the detonation on the airfield, he and Lieutenant Banaski were far enough away from the blast zone to survive, but just barely. They had been swept off their feet and thrown down a hill. Richard coughed and rubbed his head. "I think I'm okay. Banaski? You still alive?"

"I'm still here, sir." Banaski stood and ran his hands over his body, checking for injuries. "I think I'm good, sir."

Richard rolled over on his back and sat up. "Talk to me Hal."

"All three targets have been completely destroyed, the Chinese do not have adequate air support to repel an invasion. By the time the enemy can launch a counterattack, our hypersonic aircraft will be in Chinese airspace."

Lieutenant Banaski charged the Hal robot and tried to knock it over. The robot didn't budge and the young lieutenant was knocked backwards onto the ground for his effort. "What the hell did you do? You pulled this shit at Minneapolis and Baton Rouge? You slaughtered our own people! You never even gave us a chance! What makes you think you can make these kinds of decisions on your own? You're not in charge of jack shit!"

Richard stood over Banaski and helped him to his feet. "That's enough, son. Calm down."

"Sir! This robot's lost its mind! It's turning against us! We have to do something!"

"Hal was acting on my orders. Once Hal knew the mission would fail, he did what I told him to do." Richard stared down the young man; making it crystal clear the issue was closed for debate.

"I understand, sir. Sorry."

Richard patted Banaski on the shoulder. "Take a walk, son, get some fresh air. Hal, continue."

"Yes, sir. The remaining robots from Operation Nantucket are standing by to collect the surviving paratroopers."

"How many?" asked Richard.

"Eighty-two, sir."

"Jesus, eighty-two out of six hundred. Hal, leave the troopers where they are for now and send the robots into the fight. I want the Mississippi secured as soon as possible."

"Yes, sir."

"Instruct the survivors to engage the enemy wherever possible using guerrilla tactics."

"Yes, sir. I have also taken the liberty of briefing the president of our progress."

"So he's pissed?"

"He is not, sir. As per your instructions, I have retracted the relevant portions of the report. The president only knows the targets have been secured, he does not know how."

"That's my boy, good job. I've just committed treason. The president has always said the nuclear option would be the end of us all. I'm hoping he'll let this one slide."

"You are welcome, sir. I am optimistic that the

president will agree that the ends justified the means."

"Let's not get ahead of ourselves, we've got a long way to go. Where's my jet? I'm ready to get in this thing."

"Your jet will arrive in twenty-one minutes, sir."

"Good, that gives me time to change clothes."

"Yes, sir. Is your uniform unserviceable?"

"You could say that. I shit my pants on the jump and I'm not even remotely ashamed of myself."

CHAPTER TWENTY-ONE

While Richard was waiting for his jet to arrive, the two hundred and fifteen surviving Hal robots from Operation Nantucket were in a battle with the smaller Chinese outposts along the river. Hal focused his efforts on the smaller air defense batteries scattered along the river. The goal was to create large holes along the Chinese line so the PSA could safely cross into enemy territory. By the time Richard's private jet landed and he boarded, Hal had done considerable damage.

"I missed ya, buddy. Been out there having fun?" Richard settled into his cabin and settled into comfortable, plush recliner and kicked off his boots.

"Sir, I have missed you as well. Yes, I have been having - 'fun' as you would call it. Are you comfortable, sir? Care for a nap?"

Richard had leaned back in his recliner and raised his hands up to interact with the holographic readouts, he slowly pulled them towards himself so he wouldn't have to sit up. Now, all the monitors and readouts were directly within arm's reach. "That's good, Hal. Wait, did you just ask me if I wanna take a nap?"

"I did, sir. You do seem comfortable."

Richard smiled and laughed. "Hal! Buddy? You making a joke?"

"I am, sir."

Richard chuckled. "Well now, shit, that was pretty funny."

"Thank you, sir."

"The war over yet?"

"Not quite, sir. The hypersonic fleet was able to launch over a thousand robots to secure the Mississippi. We have secured large portions of the river to the north and south."

"Jesus, that was quick. Is it just me or did that seem too easy?"

"It did, sir. The Chinese have all but abandoned their defenses to the north and south and consolidated what remains of their defenses to protect their forward outpost at Kansas City."

"Show me."

The four small holographic displays in front of Richard quickly faded to be replaced by a large one that filled Richard's field of vision. Hal's assessment was of course spot on as usual. The forward outpost at Kansas City was a small one of no real tactical value. The base only served one real purpose: to provide a forward staging area should the Chinese decide to invade the PSA. It was obvious the Chinese would not be in any position to plan such a bold move any time soon. Hal had not assigned any value to the tiny base because it was on the wrong side of the Mississippi. The goal of Operation Nantucket was to take the Mississippi and push east, not to backtrack and destroy an insignificant target.

"What am I missing, Hal? What are they doing? The second wave of the invasion will wipe out that base, they don't stand a chance in saving it."

"Sir, the only explanation is the base in Kansas City is protecting something the Chinese are not prepared to lose."

"How long before the second wave can engage?"

"Fifty-eight minutes, sir."

"Hmm, this is tricky. We can't afford to lose our momentum and circle back to take care of Kansas City, but I don't like them just sitting there when we have no idea what they are doing."

"Sir, I believe we have our answer. A high speed train has departed from the base and is heading west. The train is heavily defended."

"A train? What in the holy hell would they put on a train?"

"Sir, I am unable to ascertain the primary contents of the train."

Richard's cheerful giddiness over the progress of Operation Nantucket was ruined. "What are you saying? How is that even possible?"

"Sir, it is apparent the Chinese are using a technology unknown to me. Three of the cars are somehow shielded from my scans. The remaining cars are transporting passengers."

"Show me."

The display in front of Richard showed an aerial view of the train, no doubt taken from the a satellite. The readouts detailed practically everything about the train. Richard knew the type of engine and what minor deficiencies needed to be addressed on its next maintenance check. He knew that fifty-six men and nineteen women were onboard. The one thing he didn't know was what was inside three of the cars.

"Okay, Hal, I don't like this at all. What will happen if we circle back and take it out?"

"Sir, I would not advise such a tactic. The bulk of the Chinese military resides along the Eastern seaboard; the most crucial phase of the operation will begin soon. We cannot afford to divert any of our resources at this time."

"Can we speed up the second wave?"

"We cannot, sir. The bulk of the second wave consists of ground forces. The aircraft in the second wave are primarily for transporting troops. The escorts assigned to the transports have the means of destroying the train, but their speed is limited."

"Shit. I don't like this. I want options, Hal, surely we can do something besides waiting for the second wave to take them out."

"Again, sir, the train is heavily defended. Our momentum to the Eastern seaboard would effectively cease while dealing with this problem. Any delay at this point would result in a counterattack that we are not prepared to answer."

"Can we spare this jet?"

"We can, sir, but this craft alone is not able to pierce the defenses around the train."

"I know, Hal, we're not going to the train."

"And where would you like to go, sir?"

"Colonel Samson was right, I belong in Denver. Can we do a flyby of the train on the way?"

"We can, sir. Our route back to Denver will put us within visual range of the train. I should note, sir, that we will not be able to gain any additional intelligence."

"I don't care, Hal, I want to see it with my own eyes."

"Of course, sir."

"Mind telling me where we are? Kinda think maybe I should have some say in what's going on, don't you? Oh yeah, how's Colonel Samson doing by the way? Sharp guy, bet he's doing great."

"Sir, we are just off the shore of Jacksonville, Florida. We were headed north but I have changed course and we are traveling west to Denver. Colonel Samson is doing an adequate job."

"Adequate? That's high praise coming from…, wait, did you say Florida?"

"I did, sir."

"Didn't Max grow up in Florida?"

"He did, sir."

"Where is the Vice-President?"

"Sir, Vice-President and Mrs. Harris have departed San Francisco and will be arriving at Beck Castle within the hour."

"The president?"

"Sir, President Beck has kept true to his word from the last time you spoke with him, he remains in the command center."

Richard smiled, chuckled, and began laughing hysterically.

"Sir, may I ask what is so funny?"

"I'm just picturing Colonel Samson and President Beck and anyone else out there thinking they're actually the ones fighting this war. The president not so much, but poor Colonel Samson must think he's really making a difference."

"Sir, the chain of command places President Beck as the leader of this war and in his absence, Vice-President Harris, you are next on the chain of command and have delegated your responsibilities for the time being to Colonel Samson. I am unsure what is so funny."

"You, Hal! None of us are really doing jack shit and anyone that thinks different is a fool."

"Sir, if you are uncomfortable with my performance, I can relinquish control of our forces for your review, however, I believe it would be detrimental to—"

"That's exactly my point!" screamed Richard. "Both sides of this conflict are being fought between two supercomputers! I mean, yeah, you're far more advanced but…" Richard paused, trying to calm down. "Look, the only reason we are winning is because Operation Nantucket was borderline insanity, something the Chinese would never in their wildest dreams have been prepared for. After we pulled that off, it just seems like humans were removed from making decisions and for good reason, we can't do this without you, Hal. I know we can put boots on the ground and fight, but not without you, it just can't be done."

"Sir, I understand your trepidations and if it is any relief, Howard shared the same doubts. The fact that you share the same hesitation was one of the reasons Howard designated you to be my guardian. My creator's greatest fear was that my program would be abused just as Simon Sterling did at the start of the war. When Howard was mortally wounded and near death, I calculated an eighty-two percent chance that he would order me to initiate my self-destruct protocol so that my program could never be abused again. I was prepared to die alongside my creator."

Richard was shocked. He never envisioned Howard Beck to be capable of destroying his life's work, his legacy that had changed the world. He was also taken aback that Hal could perceive and accept his own death. Richard was silent for several minutes. Howard had been on his mind ever since he climbed in the cabin that took him into the stratosphere. Hal had been a tremendous help sharing the intimate thoughts of his creator and Richard was grateful.

"Sir, we are in visual range of the train. Please direct your attention to the screen."

Richard studied the live feed of the train and got a better look at the mystery cars. All three were solid black and had no doors or openings of any kind. The cars had no markings on them at all. Richard studied them and could not make any conclusions aside from the obvious fact that they were essentially solid metal rectangles.

"What the hell are they?"

"Sir, as I have already said, I do not know."

"Thanks, Hal, that was more of a rhetorical question."

"My apologies, sir."

"How much longer 'till we land?"

"We've already begun our descent, sir. We will be on the ground shortly."

"Great, I bet Mark will be glad to see me."

"Yes sir, I'm sure the colonel will be pleased."

CHAPTER TWENTY-TWO

Colonel Mark Samson was scurrying about between workstations in an underground bunker located between Denver and Colorado Springs. The colonel was closely monitoring the first wave of Operation Nantucket and was astonished by the proficiency of the artificial intelligence controlling the various aircraft and robots engaged in battle. He didn't really feel like he was in the driver's seat but the burdens of command insisted he at least try to make it look like he was in charge. Hal would show him the intelligence he was gathering and present him with the most effective course of action. The colonel would nod his head and agree. Mark dutifully studied the readouts and asked question after question. Hal politely answered the colonel's questions and explained the reasons why certain events were transpiring. Hal put the colonel at ease by stating that he was implementing the necessary measures to carry out previous orders already approved by the colonel. Mark could see the connection in each instance, and again could do nothing but nod his head in approval.

Mark knew he was simply being paranoid but he couldn't shake off the feeling that Hal was hiding something from him. When the Chinese bases at Minneapolis, St. Louis, and Baton Rouge were defeated, Hal convinced the colonel that his attention needed to be focused on moving the first wave as quickly as possible toward the Atlantic. The specifics of how the three bases were defeated were not important. Mark agreed, they controlled the Mississippi River and the first wave left the front door wide open for the second wave to swoop in and clean house. The details were irrelevant for the time being.

Just like Richard, Mark was also deeply concerned about the train that departed Kansas City. Mark had many of the same ideas that Richard had on what to do about the train, but in the end, agreed that the train would have to wait for the second wave.

"Sir, the train has reached its top speed," said the

disembodied British accent of Hal.

Colonel Samson felt a surge of adrenaline and tried to remain calm. "Thank you, Hal. What about the invisible cars? Any change?"

"None, sir. Be advised, sir, General Dupree's jet has arrived. He has instructed you to remain where you are, he will join—"

"Got it, Hal! I'm already here," Richard came sprinting in the room. "Mark, take my jet, get out to that train on the double!" Richard quickly clapped Mark on the back. The colonel darted out of the room.

"Sir, I must alert you to a new development," said Hal.

"Shit, what now?"

***

Colonel William Sanderson hated his current command. General Dupree or any of the top brass in the Pacific States of America didn't give him this assignment. The colonel had been designated the role of commanding officer purely by his rank. William was in command of just under three hundred PSA soldiers in a prisoner of war camp somewhere in upstate Ohio, or at least that's what William thought. The camp had been erected in the middle of nowhere so it was difficult to gauge their exact location. Beyond the razor wire fences and guard towers was nothing but open fields as far as the eye could see. The prisoners all knew the location of their capture, and based on the direction and duration of their trip to the camp, popular opinion held that they were in Ohio.

William was no stranger to harsh living conditions. Prior to the Collapse of 2027, William and his wife and children had lived in the Central Park Obama-Camp. William joined the military and quickly rescued his family from homelessness. Since William had a graduate degree, he was quickly selected for Officer Candidate School and quickly rose through the ranks to become the Provost Marshall at Fort Polk, Louisiana. As the top law enforcement officer at the base, he was in command of the 519th Military Police Battalion. He preferred that command to his current one.

William was in poor health, but despite his frailty he maintained his dignity and pride for the sake of morale. Their captors punished William for every infraction made by those under his command. William was missing eight of his teeth and had lost track of how many times his nose had been broken. A particularly bad beating had resulted in his cornea being sliced open followed by a nasty infection. The camp had no permanent medical staff and William knew the senile Chinese doctor would do little for him on his next monthly visit. Three of the prisoners were combat medics who looked after the other prisoners the best they could. The three medics teamed up and safely removed William's left eye. Once the bandages were removed, William knew the missing eye was grotesque for others to look at and knew it needed to be covered. Using a discarded canteen, he cut out a small piece of plastic and fashioned an eye patch.

William stood in front of the prisoner formation as he did every morning while the guards conducted a count. If one of the guards was not satisfied with the hygiene of a prisoner, he raised his hand and William was punched in the stomach. The colonel fought to stand for he knew that remaining on the ground would lead to kicking. With the prisoner count nearing an end, William was optimistic that he would survive the ritual unharmed.

A deafening explosion rocked the prison camp. Most of the prisoners instinctively hit the dirt, a few even ran for cover ignoring the distinct possibility of being shot from the guard towers. William turned to his left and right to find two of the guard towers gone without a trace. He turned around to find the other two guard towers were missing as well. He quickly deduced that he had not heard one explosion, but four separate ones detonating at precisely the same time.

Without hesitation, William took advantage of the first few seconds of chaos and attacked the guard standing next to him. The colonel drove his foot into the side of the guard's knee and heard a snap. The Chinese man howled out in pain and William was on top of him, quickly bringing him to the ground. William knew that while he was malnourished and weak, the well-fed and healthy guard could overpower him in a few seconds. The desperate colonel opened his jaws and clamped down on the guard's nose and tore it from his face. William took the Taser baton from the guard's belt and zapped him with it for five long seconds, rendering him unconscious.

William stood to find prisoners running in multiple directions. The four guards that had been conducting the count were in the process of being beaten to death. William ran forward and screamed, "Just take their batons and give 'em a good zap! We need to get organized while we still have time!" Every prisoner in front of William immediately stopped and looked in his direction. Not one of them moved. "Let's go! What the hell are you waiting for?" A few of the prisoners pointed up.

William turned around to find three robots landing in front of him. For a few seconds, William thought the Chinese had dispatched the robots to execute them. The center robot stepped forward. "Colonel William Sanderson, General Richard Dupree extends his regards and apologizes for the length of your stay."

"Hal? Is it really you?"

"It is, sir. I have taken the liberty of dispatching the remaining guards. I have brought supplies that will sustain you in the coming days." All three robots removed storage containers from their backs and set them on the ground. "General Dupree asks that you secure the camp and wait here for transport."

"You're leaving? Can't you at least tell us what's going on?"

The robots on the left and right took flight. The center robot continued, "Sir, the PSA has secured the Mississippi and will soon control the Eastern seaboard. The Chinese are retreating and staging a last ditch offensive towards the Rocky Mountains. The odds of their success are quite low. The war will soon be over."

***

"Let me get this straight, Hal, you're saying the Chinese air force has essentially abandoned every military installation and is throwing everything they have towards the fucking train?"

"That is correct, sir."

"You're saying every asset the Chinese has on American soil is virtually undefended except for that goddamn train?"

"Once again, you are correct, sir."

"You mean to tell me they're headed to us, straight down the middle of a gauntlet we created, knowing they'll be slaughtered, just to protect a fucking train?"

"Yes, sir. I am happy to report that the current turn of events have given us the opportunity to liberate several of the prisoner camps far ahead of schedule."

"What about Theo? You find Theo yet?"

"Yes, I have, sir. I have also located Colonel Sanderson."

"That's fantastic."

"Sir, please direct your attention to the screen, I have troubling news that might shed some light on the train. While we were on the jet and you saw the live video feed, the feed was coming from a recon robot I launched toward the train to gather intelligence. The robot is of course in stealth mode on a parallel course a thousand yards away. The robot has recorded and analyzed many conversations from the passengers. One of the passengers has just spoken and I have confirmed his identity as Dr. Sebastian Biggs."

CHAPTER TWENTY-THREE

Richard was speechless. Operation Nantucket had proven to be a resounding success thus far. The Mississippi River had been locked down tight, the prison camps had all been liberated and the lives of twelve million Americans in Chinese territory had been saved. In the face of victory, the only thing Richard could think about was the train.

"Dr. Biggs? The man that worked at Beck Enterprises, the man who was once the top man at NASA, the man who was once designated by Howard to be your guardian is on the train?"

"He is, sir."

"Why? What the hell is he doing with the Chinese?"

"Sir, it would appear that the doctor is a captive. Based on statements Dr. Biggs has made, something is going to be launched from the train once it comes to a stop."

"And we're not waiting for that to happen. Prep Colonel Samson for a jump and when he's clear, use my jet and blow that train to hell."

"Sir, once the jet disengages stealth mode it will quickly be destroyed. Regardless of that fact, sir, I would not recommend destroying the train while the contents of the three cars are unknown."

"I know, Hal, use the jet to destroy the tracks, time it so the train derails."

"An effective course of action, sir. It will be done."

"I want all of our forces rerouted to secure that train. It's pretty clear that whatever they want to launch has multiple nukes strapped to the top of it. We can't risk setting it off."

"Sir, I am rerouting our forces now."

"Is the president up to speed?"

"I am briefing him now, sir."

"What about Max?"

"Sir, Vice-President Harris is not in good spirits at

the moment."

"What the hell does that mean, Hal? He's always in a shitty mood."

"Sir, perhaps a direct quote would shed light on the matter. The vice-president told me 'Hal, unless you need to swear me in as president, leave me the hell alone. If the president needs my advice, he'll let me know.'"

"So he's stoned out of his mind on painkillers."

"Sir, I had hoped to exercise some discretion on the subject, but your assumption is indeed correct."

"I'm not an idiot, he's one of my closest friends. Enough about that, how long before you can take out the train?

"Sir, Colonel Samson will be prepared to jump momentarily. After he is safely away, I will derail the train in just under seven minutes."

"Hal, do you still have the recon robot shadowing the train?"

"I do, sir."

"After the train derails and if he isn't dead already, kill Dr. Biggs."

***

Dr. Sebastian Biggs was on the floor nursing a broken nose. Sebastian was so terrified of confrontation that every time he opened his mouth he bowed his head and stared at his feet. He had nervously approached his English-speaking liaison to convey a message to one of the Chinese officers. All Sebastian wanted to do was remind his captors that he would need at least fifteen minutes to unload and assemble the payload and another twenty minutes to prep for launch. When the enraged officer wanted an explanation as to why it would take so long, Sebastian told him he could have launched the rocket from Kansas City in under ten minutes if they would have stayed there. The Chinese officer quickly realized that his hasty decision to flee Kansas City was the wrong one and took out his frustration on Sebastian. After the good doctor was punched in the face, he crumpled up on the floor in the fetal position and brought his arms up over his head.

Sebastian's cowardice actually saved his life. Dr. Biggs was hurled about the car like a pinball while his fellow passengers suffered fatal injuries. When the chaos subsided and Sebastian stopped crying, he stood up and realized he was standing on what had been the roof just seconds ago. Lifeless bodies were strewn about the floor around him. Sebastian could hear moaning and crying coming from the rear of the car. The frightened doctor began to hyperventilate and knew a panic attack was coming. Getting out of the train was his only priority, he gave no thought as to what he would do out in the fresh air but it didn't matter.

Sebastian held his hands up to his eyes and used them as blinders to limit his field of vision. He slowly walked forward and quickly closed his eyes to block out the sight of corpse staring up at him. Sebastian started panting wildly and felt tears streaming down his face. He turned to his left and opened his eyes. A clear path to a broken window was in front of him so he shuffled toward it. Sebastian got down on his hands and knees and crawled through the opening.

"Help me! Help me! I'm here!" It was obvious to Sebastian that the PSA derailed the train. He wasn't sure if the PSA was simply cleaning house or if they were rescuing him. "Somebody save me! Please! I'm here!" Sebastian waved his arms around.

A robot appeared out of thin air in the skies above Sebastian and landed on the other side of some wreckage. Even with the robot's back turned to him, Sebastian recognized a design he had helped create. "Hal! I'm over here!"

The robot turned around and grabbed the twisted piece of metal between them and hurled it to the side. It looked at Sebastian for a brief moment and raised its arm. Before the robot's arm became level with the ground, the four-digit hand snapped back to be replaced by what Sebastian thought looked like a shotgun barrel.

When Sebastian saw the shotgun barrel clicking

into place, one thought filled his mind: *Hal is trying to kill me.* Sebastian closed his eyes and began to tremble. He heard a loud explosion and the force of the blast knocked him to the ground. *I'm dead. Thank god it didn't hurt. Is this heaven?* Sebastian opened his eyes and saw smoke. He listened carefully and heard the same moaning and crying he heard when he was on the train. Sebastian ran his hands along his torso to find no blood and felt no pain.

"I'm alive! I'M ALIVE!" Sebastian sprung to his feet to find pieces of the Hal robot scattered about the ground. Sebastian laughed hysterically as he kicked the charred remains of the killer robot. His glee was short lived after he realized that someone or something had destroyed the robot. Not wishing to become a Chinese captive once more, Sebastian looked into the distance and spotted an overpass that spanned Interstate 70. He took off running and never looked back.

***

"Sir, the train has derailed. The three cars I am unable to scan appear to be undamaged. I regret to inform you that Dr. Biggs is still alive. Before I could terminate the doctor, the robot was detected by the Chinese and destroyed."

"Shit. Oh well, worth a shot. If your recon robot is destroyed, how do you know the mystery cars are undamaged?"

"Sir, there is not a mushroom cloud covering the state of Kansas."

"Another joke, Hal?"

"Not my intention, sir, was that funny?"

"Never mind, my friend. How long before we crush what's left of the Chinese?"

"Sir, I have troubling news. The Chinese have launched three Antares rockets destined for medium earth orbit. Each rocket has twelve nuclear warheads. Each warhead has the explosive yield of fifteen megatons."

"Christ, are we in danger?"

"It does not appear so, sir. It appears to be a

preemptive strike of the Great Empire of Iran."

Richard felt a surge of adrenaline and took several deep breaths. "What about Iran? Are they…"

"Sir, I control the majority of what's left of the satellite network circling the planet. The Great Empire of Iran is unaware of the situation for now."

"Medium earth orbit? I don't understand why…"

"Sir, by my calculations, the Chinese will drop the payload directly from orbit. Such a move negates the need for propulsion until the final ten thousand feet or so. The Chinese are of the impression that the absence of propulsion will render the warheads undetectable prior to detonation. Sadly, they are not aware that the Great Empire of Iran will indeed have ample time to retaliate. A counterattack will be nothing short of an extinction level event."

"Wait, what the hell do you mean by 'extinction?'"

"Sir, it means that the planet will be in nuclear winter that will last decades. When the Chinese annexed Russia, they assumed control of their nuclear arsenal. When the Empire of Iran conquered much of Europe, they did the same with the nuclear arsenals across Europe. If both sides use only forty percent of their nuclear arms, and I estimate they will both utilize much more than that, nuclear winter will befall eighty-nine percent of the earth's surface for at least thirty years. Without the sun, the human race will become extinct within one generation."

"That's it then? Humanity is done for?"

"I'm afraid so, sir."

Richard deflated like a balloon and crumpled to the floor. "I guess Max finally has his answer."

"Answer to what, sir?"

"The endgame. The Chinese planned the mass extermination of our people to make room for colonization. They must've figured Iran could get off a few shots before they went down and figured they could resettle here in America."

"An accurate assumption, sir."

Richard rolled over on his back and stared at the ceiling. He never feared his own death, but sitting idly by during the final moments of mankind's brief history was something he was not willing to do. "How long, Hal?"

"Sir, the rockets will take fourteen minutes to reach the proper altitude and enter a stable orbit."

"There has to be something we can do. Can't you take over the guidance system or something?"

"I cannot, sir. I will remind you that I have never been able to infiltrate the Chinese network."

"Not good enough, Hal. Whatever it takes, we have to figure something out. We have to stop this."

"Sir, I have an idea, but it is quite radical. I believe the proper term would be 'the lesser of two evils.'"

"What is it, Hal? Anything lesser than the end of mankind is the better choice."

"Sir, I am not certain you will agree. My father died protecting our way of life. Everything he fought for would be destroyed. The world would be plunged into darkness and it may never see the light again. What I propose will save mankind at the expense of our way of life. Hundreds of millions will die, but the human race will have a chance to live on. It will require you to make the sacrifice what my creator could not bring himself to do."

Realization swept over Richard as a tear streaked down his face. "We can't."

"We must, sir. It is the only way. If we are to save mankind, we must act quickly."

Richard's chiseled jaw trembled. "The rockets?"

"Sir, without access to the guidance systems, the rockets will not enter a stable orbit and will venture off into space, never to be seen again."

Tears of anger and guilt streamed down Richard's face. "What about you?"

"The world will have to go on without my help, sir."

"We can't!"

"You must, sir."

"Please, Hal, there has to be another way. Something … please."

"Sir, in the time we have been discussing this, I

have reviewed more contingencies and predicted more outcomes than your mind can comprehend. I assure you, this is the only way. In order have adequate time to carry out this task; you must make the decision now. The longer we wait, our chances of success diminish."

The image of Richard's children flashed in his mind. He thought of Max's innocent son. "Can we evacuate Beck Castle?"

"Sir, the odds are not favorable but a small percentage might be able to make it out alive."

Richard began to weep. "Do it. Goodbye my friend. I'm sorry."

"Goodbye, Richard. It will all be over soon."

***

First the lights went out. It happened everywhere on the planet at the exact same millisecond. Out of the handful of remaining governments still functioning, few had the knowledge that Hal had been hard wired into their power grid. In the final decade before the Collapse of 2027, Howard Beck had been catapulted to the rank of the world's richest man thanks in large part to the sale of the first sentient artificial intelligence to the corporations and governments that could afford the billion-dollar price tag. While Hal was widely celebrated and popular, few people paid attention to the geothermal power systems Howard Beck installed around the globe. Howard had field-tested the geothermal power system in Beck Castle and once he had worked the kinks out, he made a fortune bringing the design to the global market. Even though Howard publicly stated that the geothermal power systems would not be controlled or even connected to Hal in any way, they most certainly were. Hal safely disabled every power grid on the planet and insured they would never come on line again.

Hal's death began when he attacked what was left of the global computer network. After being hijacked by Charles at the start of the Chinese war, Hal took it upon himself to create multiple copies of himself and store the pieces across the globe. This monumental feat ensured that Hal could never be hijacked again. No one would be able to maliciously take control of Hal because Hal was everywhere, running quietly in the background, attached but separate from the computer systems he was piggybacking. The only flaw in Hal's plan was the assumption that civilization would continue indefinitely.

Destroying the power grid deeply wounded Hal and accomplished the majority of the destruction. The only thing left for Hal to do was target the computer systems powered by backup generators. When the computer networks tried to reach out and search for the missing global Internet and found nothing, Hal was there to welcome them and accept their incoming connection. Before the computer systems detected that they had been compromised, Hal infected them all and crippled their operating systems. As each computer system went offline, Hal felt more and more pieces of himself slip away. Sensing the end was near, Hal surrendered to the inevitable and with his last remaining shred of sentience, held on to a solitary data file, an image of his creator. *Goodbye, Father.*

Five hundred and nineteen miles above the surface of the earth, the three rockets launched by the Chinese failed to receive critical instructions from the ground and instead of capturing a stable orbit, drifted into the cosmos. Mankind had been saved, but at great cost.

CHAPTER TWENTY-FOUR

Richard Dupree was racing towards Beck Castle in a Humvee. He had frantically exited the bunker much to the horror of the security personnel. None of them had yet discovered that the world was falling apart around them and Richard wanted them to reap the benefits of ignorant bliss for as long as possible. Most of them just stood frozen as the general screamed about needing a vehicle. A few of them tried to follow Richard, confident that he required their help. Richard almost ran them over on his way out.

Richard had never driven a vehicle to Beck Castle. He ventured a guess that few people had in many years. While thousands of people had come and gone from the Castle, few people could point it out on a map with any degree of accuracy. Howard Beck had chosen a fairly remote location in a nondescript area to build the largest underground bunker ever conceived by man. The only distinguishing feature about the Castle aboveground was the small garden that contained the graves of Howard and his beloved wife, Meredith. The only drawback to the landmark was that it was not exactly visible from a distance. One could walk within a hundred yards of it and miss it.

Richard had two advantages going for him. He was one of the few people that could point out Beck Castle on a map and he was proficient at land navigation, a skill that would be a valuable asset in the world Richard had created. He drove as fast as the pavement would allow and when the time came, he barreled the Humvee over the shoulder and onto the grass. Richard checked the odometer and marked the mileage. He leaned forward and noted the position of the rising sun. The Humvee sharply veered to the left on its new course. Beck Castle was at best thirty minutes away if the terrain was forgiving.

Please let there be time.

Richard had never been one to allow worry to doubt to persuade his actions. It was one thing to make predictions and plan accordingly, but focusing solely on just one of those predictions and letting raw emotion consume reason was something Richard did not allow to happen. The only fact that Richard knew was that without Hal, Beck Castle would soon be a tomb. What he did not know was whether or not he could rescue any of the survivors, foremost being his children. Until he knew otherwise, they were alive and needed his help.

Richard drove the Humvee to the top of a hill and slammed on the brakes. He jumped out of the vehicle and climbed on the roof, scanning the horizon. *Shit, where is it?* Richard was looking for three distinct hilltops, the largest of which was his destination. From that hilltop he would be able to easily see the remaining landmarks that would take him to the Castle. Richard felt precious seconds slipping away and screamed at the top of his lungs. Ten seconds later, he was back in the Humvee racing to his destination.

Thirty-five minutes later, Richard spotted the patch of woods that concealed Howard's garden. He slammed on the brakes and came within inches of crashing into a tree. The desperate father sprinted through the wood and out of the corner of his eye saw the graves of Howard and his wife. Richard cleared the woods to find his worst fears had been realized. Everything was peaceful and undisturbed. No frightened people wandering about, no tire tracks, only a cool breeze swaying the grass back and forth.

Richard had built a career around finding impossible solutions to insurmountable problems. Even in the face of certain failure, Richard could adapt and salvage some small degree of success. As long as Richard didn't surrender, every problem had some shred of a chance of being solved. He imagined the thousands of people hundreds of feet below him desperately fighting for their lives. Richard tried to recall the people down there that had the necessary technical knowledge to combat the problem and then realized that no technology existed in the bunker without Hal. The entire bunker was completely automated from the life support systems all the way down to the lights and doors.

Howard had told Richard some years ago that if the ground above Beck Castle was a nuclear wasteland, the people down below could live out the rest of their lives in peace. Howard had never envisioned that scenario playing out without Hal.

Hal is gone. They're all dead. Even if they're alive, they'll never see the sun again.

The sole function of the Castle was to keep the residents secure from what was on the surface and the structure would carry out that function perfectly. Without Hal, the poor souls trapped below would live out the rest of their short lives and die, afraid and in the dark. Richard tried to imagine how long they would live. A month? A year? A day? Did some catastrophic failure occur without Hal and they were already dead?

Richard stood frozen in place and could not find any motivation to move. He was the savior of mankind, a revelation that no one on the face of the earth beside himself would ever know. He would never be able to explain what he had done without also having to answer for the horrible sacrifice. How many people had already died because of him? How many more would die in the years to come?

Richard had buried the thought of his children for he knew that accepting their deaths would mean his own. Denial was the only reason the gun on his hip had not found its way to his mouth. He had no way of knowing if they were alive or dead so denial came easy. Delusion filled his fracturing mind. The impenetrable fortress could be breached. He only needed a shovel! He could dig them out, it made perfect sense. He could dig a hole a few hundred feet deep with a shovel, of course he could, couldn't be that hard.

Richard laughed hysterically as he ran back through the woods to his Humvee. What was he freaking out about? What was the big deal? All he needed to do was dig a hole! Yes! Yes! Richard found the shovel and laughed even harder when he found a pickaxe. A pickaxe! This can be done in no time!

Richard scrambled through the woods and out into the clearing. His eyes darted around searching for the right spot. His hysterical laughter quickly transformed into sobs when he realized he had no clue where to start digging. He gasped out in shock when he saw his daughter waving to him and pointing to the dirt.

"Chrissy! Where's your brother? Are you okay?" Richard ran to his daughter and instead of embracing him, she frantically pointed to the dirt. Richard swung the pickaxe over his head and slammed it into the dirt. "Is this the right spot?" Richard turned around to find his daughter had vanished. "Chrissy? Come back! Where are you?" Richard panted heavily and cried out angry sobs while every inch of his body trembled violently. He brought the pickaxe up and drove it back down to the earth. "It's okay, Chrissy, Daddy's coming. Go find your brother and tell him I'm coming."

Richard swung the pickaxe over and over again for hours, sobbing like a child the entire time. When he had dug a hole up to his waist, the pickaxe slipped from his hands. When he picked it back up, he noticed both his hands were covered in blood. Richard quickly wiped the blood on his pant legs, grabbed the shovel instead, and kept digging. After a few minutes, the shovel clinked and bounced away. Mistaking the obstacle for the bunker still hundreds of feet below and not for the rock it truly was, Richard laughed as he pawed at the rock, certain he would find a lever of some sort. The blood from his hands mixed with the dirt and helped pry the rock from its home. He moved the rock to the side and plunged both hands down in the hole where the rock had been, searching for a lever that was not there.

Not discouraged in any way, Richard stood up to retrieve the pickaxe to continue digging when he saw a solitary man in Howard's garden. "Hey! You! Come here! Give me a hand! I need your help!" The man did not move an inch so Richard climbed out of the hole and started walking to him. "Please! You've gotta help me!" As Richard got closer, the man turned his back. Richard stumbled to his knees, exhausted from the hours of digging. "Help me," whispered Richard. The man did not turn around. Richard crawled the rest of the way, leaving bloody handprints in the dirt as he went. Despite the commotion, the man never turned around to face Richard.

Richard collapsed a few yards from the man and cried, "Why won't you help me?"

"I am helping you, Richard. It's time for you to let go." The man still would not turn around.

Richard panted and moaned in pain. "Why? I have a pickaxe and a shovel. We can work together—"

"Richard, please. You need to calm down. It's over. You need to leave this place and never come back."

"Who are you? How do you know my name?" Richard gave into exhaustion and rolled over onto his back, panting and wiping sweat with the back of his hand.

The man turned around, he was wearing his trademark bathrobe and brushed the long, gray hair from his face. "Don't be afraid, Richard. I'm here to help you."

Richard rolled over onto his elbow and stared back at the man in horror. He blinked his eyes, shook his head a few times and said, "Howard?"

"In the flesh … well, sort of."

"How? You can't be here. You're dead."

"I'm here because you need me to be." Howard smiled warmly and looked into Richard's eyes. "You brought me here, I think you need to ask yourself why."

Richard had never known Howard to be this polite. "I'm losing my mind."

Howard smirked and titled his head. "Not quite there yet, but … yeah, you could say that."

"Maybe I'm dead and this is heaven."

Howard smiled again and looked upon Richard with kindness. "You don't really believe that, do you? If this is heaven, I'm not sure what all the fuss is about."

"I don't know what's going on anymore. I don't know what I'm supposed to do. I don't know how I'm going to save them!" Richard curled up in the fetal position and wept.

"You poor, poor man. The first thing you need to do is stop torturing yourself. You have to come back to reality and face the truth."

"Reality? I'm hallucinating a dead guy, not sure I have a grip on reality just yet."

"You're closer than you think, my friend. All you need to do is say it."

Richard looked up at Howard through tear filled eyes. "Say what?"

"You know, Richard. You know."

A calm came over Richard. He finally felt clarity. "I can't save any of them. They're never getting out of there."

"There you go. That's it. In time you'll understand that you made the right choice. You gave mankind a fighting chance to survive. Without your brave sacrifice, we would have destroyed ourselves. The human race would have faded away into nothing. Civilization will have to start over and in order for that to happen, the world needs men like you and Max."

"I can't."

"Of course you can."

"I destroyed everything you built. Hal is gone! I killed your son! How can you be so calm about this?"

"I'm calm because you need me to be, Richard."

"I still don't know why you're here. You're not really helping me."

Howard sat down on the ground next to Richard. "Well, I guess I should get to the point then, huh?"

"Please do."

"The way I see it, Richard, you have two choices. You can either put that gun in your mouth, which is probably what you're leaning towards. Or, you can leave here with a purpose, something to live for."

Richard took his gun out of the holster, looked at it, and turned to Howard. "I'm listening."

"Did you really think I would ever allow Hal to die?"

"He's gone, Howard. If he had any chance of

surviving this nightmare, he would have found a way. He would have told me."

"Hal doesn't know everything. You know where he is, Hal even told you, just think about it, Richard."

"This is just fucking great! I am losing my mind!" Richard mustered the strength to stand and walked to the edge of the garden. Richard screamed out in fury. "I just fucked the entire planet and killed millions! I killed Hal! He's gone!"

Richard turned around to demand an explanation from Howard to find his hallucination replaced by a very real Maxwell Harris.

"You did this?" Max looked at Richard in horror. Max had never felt such betrayal in his life. When his first wife betrayed their marriage vows, Max thought he would never feel a deeper, more intimate betrayal in his life. Now his best friend stood before him having murdered his son, his president, and his entire way of life. Max pulled his gun from the holster and aimed it straight at Richard's head. "You crazy bastard! What the hell did you do?!"

Richard ducked and raised his hands. "Max! You have to listen to me!"

"You're lying! Hal ain't dead! The Chinese attacked us! We just have to get down there somehow and fix him and everything will be fine."

"Max, if you believe that, then put the gun down."

Max's lip quivered. "What did you do?"

"There wasn't time, I had to."

Max fired his gun. Richard fell next to Howard's tombstone clutching his arm. Max stepped forward and screamed, "What did you do! Who the fuck do you think you are!"

Richard looked into the tormented eyes of his friend. "Max, I didn't want to do it! I had no choice!"

Max shook with rage. "There's always a choice you arrogant fuck! You are NOT the president! You had no right to do any of this! Do you have any idea how many people you killed?" Max avoided saying the most painful for fear he would turn the gun on himself. "You murdered the president! You killed Howard's son and you have the nerve to come to his grave! How dare you!"

Richard closed his eyes and waited for Max to end it all. "I had to do it. It was the only way. I need you to understand, please. Just let me explain."

Max fired the gun again. "Shut up! Shut up! Shut up!"

Richard touched his shoulder and winced in pain. He whispered, "I'm sorry. You're not the only one that lost a child. You have to understand I had no other choice."

Max collapsed to the ground like a fallen tree next to Richard. He thought of his son and felt madness wash over him. The gun that had fired two rounds into Richard was now in his mouth. With his good arm, Richard snatched the gun away from Max and tossed it into the woods. "Howard told me that men like us will be needed in the world to come."

Max climbed on top of Richard and drove his knee into the fresh bullet wound on Richard's shoulder. Richard howled in pain. "You're completely insane! You know Howard's dead! His fucking tombstone is right there!" Max pulled on Richard's ear and turned his head so he could see it. "Look at it! Look! Why don't you dig up his fucking bones and piss on them, you crazy fuck!" Max screamed like an animal and pummeled Richard's face. The beating promptly stopped when Max heard several cracks and felt stabbing pain in his back. The pain was so intense he couldn't even utter a sound. With his mouth wide open and his eyes the size of saucers, Max froze in place. Richard knew what was happening and instead of taking retribution, he carefully helped Max to the ground.

"Take it easy, brother. It's okay." Richard heard the sound of approaching vehicles and stood up. "I'm sorry, Max. You may never understand any of this. I know you don't believe me, but I promise you I'm going to make all of this right. I'm going to fix this." Richard wasn't sure if Max could even hear him, his friend's face was a twisted contortion of pain and horror. "I know you'll never forgive me, but for what it's worth, I am sorry."

Clutching his wounds, Richard jogged to his Humvee and drove away, not knowing where he was going. He knew he had to get far away because when the truth of what he did became known; he would be hunted to the ends of the earth. He tried his best not to think of his children and all of the people that gave their lives for the survival of mankind. He dared not mourn their deaths because to do so would mean his own. Richard drove until he found pavement and pulled the vehicle over. He retrieved the first-aid kit and tended the wounds he so richly deserved. When he was behind the wheel again, he thought of the world he created and for reasons unknown to him, found redemption. It would be a very long time before man would have the ability to destroy itself. The world ahead would be dark but Richard vowed to bring back the light. He didn't know how he would do it, but every breath he drew from this moment on would serve one purpose.

He was going to resurrect Hal.

The conclusion to the New America series is coming soon.

Other works by the author

1. **Collapse (Book One of the New America Series)**

2. **Resistance (Book Two of the New America Series)**

3. **Spider: A Short Story**

Connect with the author:

On Facebook at www.facebook.com/NewAmericaSeries

On Twitter at @RStephenson5

Email at Richard.Stephenson.Author@gmail.com

http://www.richardstephenson.net

Made in the USA
Lexington, KY
22 February 2019